This is for my mother, Stella, and for my House Man: NJ

THE HOUSE I LOVED

THE HOUSE I LOVED

Tatiana de Rosnay

WINDSOR
PARAGON

First published 2012
by Pan Books
This Large Print edition published 2012
by AudioGO Ltd
by arrangement with
Pan Macmillan

Hardcover   ISBN: 978 1 445 84717 7
Softcover   ISBN: 978 1 445 84718 4

British Library Cataloguing in Publication Data available

Printed and bound in Great Britain by
MPG Books Group Limited

ACKNOWLEDGMENTS

My first thanks go to historian Didier Le Fur, who initiated me into the world of the Bibliothèque Nationale, and to Véronique Vallauri, whose flower shop is the inspiration for Alexandrine's.

AUTHOR'S NOTE

Born and bred a Parisian, I love my city like most Parisians do. I have always been fascinated by its richness and history. Napoleon III and Baron Haussmann, between 1852 and 1870, gave Paris a new and much-needed modernity. They shaped the city into what it is today.

But I often wondered what it must have been like, as a Parisian, to witness those changes. And what it must have meant to lose a beloved house, like Rose does. Those eighteen years of "embellishments," before the Commune insurrection stormed the city, were no doubt hell for Parisians. Zola artfully described it, and criticized it, in *The Kill.* Victor Hugo and Baudelaire also voiced their discontent, as did the Goncourt brothers. But however much Haussmann was resented, his work remains essential to the creation of a truly modern Paris.

I have taken very few liberties with dates

and places in this novel. The rue Childebert, the rue Erfurth, the rue Taranne and the rue Sainte-Marguerite did exist, 140 years ago, within Saint-Germain-des-Prés. So did the place Gozlin, the rue Beurrière, the passage Saint-Benoît and the rue Sainte-Marthe.

The next time you walk along the boulevard Saint-Germain, go to the corner of rue du Dragon, just in front of the Café de Flore. You will notice an entire line of ancient buildings, miraculously standing between Haussmannian ones. Those are the vestiges of one side of the old rue Taranne, where the fictitious Baronne de Vresse used to live. A famous American designer has a flagship store there that could very well have been the Baronne's home. Have a look inside.

When you walk up the rue des Ciseaux, toward the church, try to ignore the noisy boulevard in front of you, and imagine the small and narrow rue Erfurth leading you straight to the rue Childebert, which used to be exactly where the metro station of Saint-Germain-des-Près now stands, on the left. And if ever you glimpse a coquettish silver-haired sexagenarian with a tall brunette on her arm, then you may just have seen Rose and Alexandrine on their way home.

TR
Paris, April 2011

Paris slashed with saber cuts, its veins opened.

— ÉMILE ZOLA,
The Kill, 1871

The old Paris is no more (the shape of a city changes faster, alas! than the human heart).

— CHARLES BAUDELAIRE,
"The Swan," 1861

I wish for all this to be marked on my body when I am dead. I believe in such cartography — to be marked by nature, not just to label ourselves on a map like the names of rich men and women on buildings.

— MICHAEL ONDAATJE,
The English Patient

My beloved,

I can hear them coming up our street. It is a strange, ominous rumble. Thuds and blows. The floor aquiver under my feet. There are shouts too. Men's voices, loud and excited. The whinny of horses, the stamp of hooves. It sounds like a battle, like in that hot and dreadful July when our daughter was born, or that bloody time when the barricades went up all over the city. It smells like a battle. Stifling clouds of dust. Acrid smoke. Dirt and rubble. I know the Hôtel Belfort has been destroyed, Gilbert told me. I cannot bear to think about it. I will not. I am relieved Madame Paccard is not here to see it.

I am sitting in the kitchen as I write this to you. It is empty, the furniture was packed up last week and sent to Tours, with Violette. They left the table behind, it was too bulky, as well as the heavy enamel cooker.

They were in a hurry and I loathed watching that being done. I hated every minute of it. The house stripped of all its belongings in one short moment. Your house. The one you thought would be safe. Oh, my love. Do not be afraid. I will never leave.

The sun peeks into the kitchen in the mornings, I've always appreciated that about this room. So dismal now, without Mariette bustling about, her face reddened by the heat of the stove, and Germaine grumbling, smoothing back wisps of hair into her tight chignon. If I try, I can almost pick up the enticing wafts of Mariette's ragout weaving its slow path through the house. Our once-cheerful kitchen is sad and bare without the gleaming pots and pans, kept scrupulously clean by Germaine, without the herbs and spices in their little glass bottles, the fresh vegetables from the market, the warm bread on its cutting board.

I remember the morning the letter came, last year. It was a Friday. I was in the sitting room, reading *Le Petit Journal* by the window, and drinking my tea. I enjoy that quiet hour before the day begins. It wasn't our usual postman. This one, I had never seen. A tall, bony fellow, his hair flaxen under the flat green cap. His blue cotton blouse with its red collar appeared far too large for him. From where I was sitting, I saw him jauntily touch his cap and hand the mail over to Germaine. Then he was gone, and I could hear his soft whistle as he marched up the street.

It was early still, I'd had my breakfast a while ago. I went back to my newspaper after a sip of tea. It seemed the Exposition Universelle was all they could talk about these past months. Seven thousand foreigners pouring through the boulevards every day. A whirl of prestigious guests: Alexander II from Russia, Bismarck, the Vice King of Egypt. Such a triumph for our Emperor.

I heard Germaine's step on the stairs. The rustle of her dress. I do not get much mail. Usually a letter from my daughter, from time to time, when she feels dutiful. Or maybe from my son-in-law, for the same reason. Sometimes a card from my brother Émile. Or from the Baronne de Vresse, in Biarritz, by the sea, where she spends her summer. And the occasional bills and taxes.

That morning I noticed a long white envelope. Closed with a thick crimson seal. I turned it around. Préfecture de Paris. Hôtel de Ville.

And my name, printed large, in black lettering. I opened it. The words leaped out.

At first I could not understand them. Yet my reading glasses were perched on the end of my nose. My hands were shaking so hard I had to place the sheet of paper on my lap and inhale a deep breath. After a while I took the letter into my hand again and forced myself to read it.

"What is it, Madame Rose?" whimpered Germaine. She must have seen my face.

I slipped the letter back into its envelope. I stood up and smoothed my dress down with the palms of my hands. A pretty frock, dark blue, with just enough ruffle for an old lady like me. You would have approved. I remember that dress, and the shoes I was wearing that day, mere slippers, sweet and feminine, and I remember Germaine's cry when I told her what the letter said.

It was not until later, much later, alone in our room, that I collapsed on the bed. Although I knew this would happen one day, sooner or later, it still came as a shock. That night, when the household was asleep, I fetched a candle and I found that map of the city you used to like to look at. I rolled it out flat on the dining room table, taking care not to spill any wax. Yes, I could see it, the inexorable northern advance of the rue de Rennes sprouting straight from the Montparnasse railway station to us, and the boulevard Saint-Germain, a hungry monster, creeping westward from the river. With two trembling fingers I traced their paths until my flesh met. Right over our street. Yes, my love, our street.

It is freezing in the kitchen, I need to go down to get another shawl. Gloves as well, but only for my left hand, as my right hand must go on writing this for you. You thought the church and its proximity would save us, my love. You and Père Levasque.

"They will never touch the church, nor the houses around it," you scoffed fifteen years ago, when the Prefect was appointed. And even after we heard what was going to happen to my brother Émile's house, when the boulevard de Sébastopol was created, you still were not afraid: "We are close to the church, it will protect us."

I often go to sit in the church to think of you. You have been gone for ten years now. A century to me. The church is quiet, peaceful. I gaze at the ancient pillars, the cracked paintings. I pray. Père Levasque comes to see me and we talk in the hushed gloom.

"It will take more than a Prefect or an Emperor to harm our neighborhood, Madame Rose! The church is safe, and so are we, its fortunate neighbors," he whispers emphatically. "Childebert, the Merovingian

King, the founder of our church, watches over his creation like a mother would a child."

Père Levasque is fond of reminding me of how many times the church has been looted, plundered and burnt down to the ground by the Normans in the ninth century. I believe it is thrice. How wrong you were, my love.

The church will be safe. But not our house. The house you loved.

The day the letter came, a feverish panic hit our little street. Monsieur Zamaretti, the bookseller, and Alexandrine, the flower girl, came up to see me. They had received the same letter from the Préfecture. But I could tell they knew it was not so bad for them. They could start their business elsewhere, could they not? There would always be a place in the city for a bookstore and a flower shop. Yes, their eyes dared not meet mine. They felt it was worse for me. As your widow, I owned the place. I let out the two shops, one to Alexandrine, the other to Monsieur Zamaretti, as you used to. As your father did before you, and his father did as well. The income from the shops was how I survived. That was how I made ends meet. Until now.

It was a warm, humid day, I recall. The street was soon humming with all our neighbors brandishing the letter. It was quite a sight. Everyone seemed to be outside that morning, and voices rose vociferously, all the way down to the rue Sainte-Marguerite. There was Monsieur Jubert, from the printing house, with his ink-stained apron, and Madame Godfin, standing outside her herbalist's shop, and there was Monsieur Bougrelle, the bookbinder, puffing away on his pipe. The racy Mademoiselle Vazembert from the haberdashery (whom you never met, thank the Lord) flounced up and down along the cobblestones, as if to flaunt her new crinoline. Our charming neighbor Madame Barou smiled sweetly when she saw me, but I could tell how distressed she was. The chocolate maker, Monsieur Monthier, appeared to be in tears. Monsieur Helder, owner of the restaurant you used to love, Chez Paulette, was nervously biting his lips, his bushy mustache moving up and down.

I had my hat on, as I never leave the house without it, but in their haste, many had forgotten theirs. Madame Paccard's bun threatened to collapse as her head waggled furiously. Docteur Nonant, hatless too, was waving an irate forefinger. At one point the wine merchant, Monsieur Horace, managed to make himself heard over the din. He has not changed much since you left us. His curly dark hair is perhaps a trifle grayer, and his paunch has no doubt swollen a mite, but his flamboyant mannerisms and loud chuckle have not faded. His eyes twinkle, black as charcoal.

"What are you ladies and gentlemen doing out here gabbling your heads off? Much good it will do us all. I'm offering the lot of you a round of drinks, even those who never come in to my den!" By that, of course, he meant Alexandrine, my flower girl, who shies away from liquor. I believe she once told me her father died a drunk.

Monsieur Horace's wine shop is damp and low-ceilinged, and has not been altered since your day. Rows and rows of bottles line the walls, hefty tubs of wine tower over wooden benches. We all gathered around the counter. Mademoiselle Vazembert took up a vast amount of space with her crinoline. I sometimes wonder how ladies live a normal life ensconced within those cumbersome contraptions. How on earth do they get into a hackney, how do they sit down for supper, how do they deal with private, natural matters? The Empress manages easily enough, I presume, as she is pampered by ladies-in-waiting who answer every whim and attend every need. I am glad to be an old woman of nearly sixty. I do not have to follow the fashions, to bother about the shape of my corsage, of my skirts. But I am rambling on, am I not, Armand? I must get on with the story. My fingers are increasingly cold. Soon I shall make some tea to warm myself up.

Monsieur Horace handed out eau de vie in surprisingly dainty glasses. I did not touch mine. Neither did Alexandrine. But no one noticed. There was much going on. Everyone compared their letters. They all had the same heading. Expropriation order by decree. We were all going to be offered a certain amount of money according to our property and our situation. Our little street, the rue Childebert, was to be utterly demolished in order to build the continuation of rue de Rennes and the boulevard Saint-Germain.

I felt that morning I was by your side, up there, or wherever it is that you are now, and that I was watching the agitation from a distance. And somehow this protected me. And it was thus, wrapped in a sort of numbness, that I listened to my neighbors and noted their different reactions. Monsieur Zamaretti's forehead glistened with sweat and he kept patting it with one of his fancy silk kerchiefs. Alexandrine was stony-faced.

"I have an excellent lawyer," gulped

Monsieur Jubert, knocking back his eau de vie with grubby, blue-stained fingers, "he will get me out of this. It is preposterous to envisage abandoning my printing house. Ten people work for me. The Prefect is not going to have the last word."

With a seductive toss of frilly petticoats, Mademoiselle Vazembert stepped forward. "But what can we do against the Prefect, against the Emperor, monsieur? They have been ripping up the city for the last fifteen years. We are but helpless."

Madame Godfin nodded, her nose bright pink. Then Monsieur Bougrelle said, very loudly, startling us all:

"Maybe there is money to be gotten out of this. Lots of it. If we play our cards right."

The room was hazy with smoke. It made my eyes sting.

"Come, now, my good man," scorned Monsieur Monthier, who had at last stopped sniveling. "The power of the Prefect and that of the Emperor is unshakable. We have witnessed enough of it to know that by now."

"Alas!" sighed Monsieur Helder, his face very red.

As I watched them all in silence, with an equally silent Alexandrine by my side, I noticed the angriest of the bunch were

Madame Paccard, Monsieur Helder and Docteur Nonant. They no doubt had the most at stake. Chez Paulette has twenty tables, and Monsieur Helder employs an entire staff to run his excellent eatery. Remember how that restaurant was never empty? How clients came all the way from the right bank to sample the exquisite blanquette? The Hôtel Belfort stands proudly on the corner of the rue Bonaparte and the rue Childebert, it boasts sixteen rooms, thirty-six windows, five stories, a fine restaurant. Losing that hotel, for Madame Paccard, meant losing the fortune of a lifetime, everything her now-deceased husband and she had strived for. The beginnings had been hard, I knew. They had worked day and night to refurbish the place, to give it the cachet it now possessed. In preparation for the Exposition Universelle, the hotel was booked solidly, week after week.

As for Docteur Nonant, never had I seen him so incensed. His usually calm face was contorted with ire.

"I will lose all my patients," he fumed, "all my clientele, everything I have built year after year. My consulting rooms are easy to get to, on the ground floor, no steep stairs, my cabinet is sunny, large, my patients approve of it. I am a step away from the hospital where I consult, on the rue Jacob. What will I do now? How can the Prefect imagine I will be satisfied with an absurd sum of money?"

What you must know, Armand, is that it was an odd feeling to be standing in that shop and listening to the others, and knowing in my heart of hearts that I did not share their wrath. I was not concerned. They were ranting about money. And they all glanced at me and expected me to speak, to voice my own fear, as a widow, about losing my two shops, and therefore losing my income. Oh, my love, how could I explain? How could I begin to tell them what this meant to me? My pain, my suffering, existed in different realms. Not money. No. It was beyond money. It was the house that I saw in my mind's eye. Our house. And how much you loved it. And what it meant to you.

In the midst of all of this racket, Madame Chanteloup, the buxom laundress from the rue des Ciseaux, and Monsieur Presson, the coal man, made a spectacular entrance. Madame Chanteloup, purple with excitement, announced she had a client who worked at the Préfecture, and that she had seen a copy of the layout and the opening of the new boulevard. The condemned streets in our vicinity were as follows: rue Childebert, rue Erfurth, rue Sainte-Marthe, rue Sainte-Marguerite, passage Saint-Benoît.

"Which means," she shrieked triumphantly, "that my laundry and Monsieur Presson's coal shop are safe. The rue des Ciseaux is not being destroyed!"

Her words were met with sighs and groans. Mademoiselle Vazembert stared at her with contempt, and swept out of the boutique, head held high. Her heels tapped down the street. I remember being shocked that the rue Sainte-Marguerite, where I was born, was also doomed. But the real anxiety, the one that gnawed at me, the one that instilled the fear that has not left me since, was about the destruction of our house. Of the rue Childebert.

It was not yet noon. Some had had a trifle too much to drink. Monsieur Monthier started to cry again, childish sobs that both repelled and touched me. Monsieur Helder's mustache once again bobbed up and down. I made my way back to our house, where Germaine and Mariette were waiting for me anxiously. They wanted to know what was going to happen to them, to us, to the house. Germaine had been to the market. Everyone was discussing the letters, the expropriation order. About what this would do to our neighborhood. The market gardener pulling his ramshackle cart had asked after me. What is Madame Rose going to do, he had demanded, where is she going to go? Both Germaine and Mariette were flustered.

I took off my hat and gloves and calmly told Mariette to get luncheon going. Something simple and fresh. A sole, perhaps, as it was Friday? Germaine beamed, she had purchased just that from the fishmonger. Mariette and she scuttled to the kitchen. And I sat down, still calm, and picked up *Le Petit Journal,* like I did every day. Only I did not make out a word of what I was reading, my fingers trembled and my heart was pumping like a drum. I kept thinking about what Madame Chanteloup had said. Her street was safe. It was a few meters away, just at the bottom of the rue Erfurth, and it was to be safe. How come? How was this possible? In whose name?

That same evening, Alexandrine came up to see me. She wished to confer about what had happened that morning and how I felt about the letter. She rushed in as usual, a whirlwind of curls and a wispy black shawl despite the heat, kindly but firmly ordered Germaine to leave us, and sat next to me.

Let me describe her to you, Armand, as I met her the year after you died. I wish you had known her. She is perhaps the only sunshine in my sad little life since you left. Our daughter Violette is no sunshine in my life. But you already know that, do you not?

Alexandrine Walcker replaced the aging Madame Colléville, as she was also in the flower trade. So young, I thought, when I saw her for the first time, nine years ago. Young and bossy. Barely twenty years old. She stamped around the shop, pouting and making scathing remarks. It is true to say that Madame Colléville had not left the place looking particularly tidy. Nor cheerful, for that matter. Never had the shop and its premises seemed drabber and darker than that morning.

Alexandrine Walcker. Surprisingly tall, bony even, yet with an unexpected lush bosom that pushed up from beneath her long black bodice. A round, pale face, almost moonlike, that made me at first fear she was daft, but how wrong I was. As soon as she set her fiery toffee-colored eyes on me, I understood. They fairly snapped with intelligence. A small, buttonlike mouth that rarely smiled. An odd, turned-up nose. And a thick mane of glossy chestnut curls elaborately piled on top of her round skull.

Pretty? No. Charming? Not quite. There was something very peculiar about Mademoiselle Walcker, I sensed that immediately. I forgot to mention her voice. Gratingly sharp. She also had the odd habit of pursing up her lips as if she were sucking on a bonbon. But I had not heard her laugh yet, you see. That took a while. Alexandrine Walcker's laugh is the most exquisite, delicious sound you have ever heard. Like the tinkle of a fountain.

She certainly had not been laughing as she glanced into the tiny, dingy kitchen area and the adjoining bedroom, so damp that the very walls seemed to exude water. She ran a finger along the moisture, glanced at it doubtfully, and said, with that sharp voice:

"Has anyone ever tried to do anything about this?"

The meek notary who was accompanying us squirmed, not daring to meet my eye.

"Well," I said brightly, "we were planning to, at one point. But Madame Colléville did not seem to bother with the damp all that much."

Alexandrine Walcker looked down at me with disdain, her eyebrows arched.

"And you are the owner, I believe. Madame . . ."

"Bazelet," I stammered. Oh, my dear, she

31

made me feel like a downright fool.

"I see. It is my belief that property owners should bother about damp. After all, you do live here as well, do you not?"

Without even waiting for my answer, she carefully made her way along the rickety steps to the cellar, where old Madame Colléville used to keep her flower stock. She seemed unimpressed by the whole place, and later I was flabbergasted to hear from our notary that she had decided to take it on.

As soon as she moved into the flower shop, a dazzling transformation took over. Remember how Madame Colléville's shop always looked gloomy, even at high noon? How her flowers seemed classical, colorless and, let me admit it, trivial? Alexandrine arrived one day with a team of workers, sturdy young fellows who made such a terrific racket — crashes, bangs and hearty laughter — all morning long that I sent Germaine down to see what the fuss was about. As Germaine ended by not coming back at all, I ventured down myself. I was astounded as I stood on the threshold.

The boutique was inundated with light. The workers had gotten rid of Madame Colléville's dreary brown drapes and gray finishings. They had scrubbed all traces of dark and damp away and were painting each wall and corner over with a luminous white. The floor had been polished and fairly gleamed. The partitions separating the shop from the back room had come down, making the place twice as large. I was greeted cheerfully by the young men and could tell why Germaine had taken her time about coming back up, as they were indeed a handsome bunch. And most jovial. Mademoiselle Walcker was in the cellar, bossing another young man around. I could hear her strident voice from where I stood.

"Oh, for heaven's sake, young man, that spot will need another go. Don't sigh like that, now, you know as well as I do the job is not finished. So get on with it, pray. We haven't got all morning."

When she saw me, she nodded curtly, and that was it. Not even, *Good day, Madame Bazelet.* I sensed I was de trop and took my leave, feeling as humble as a servant.

The following day, Germaine breathlessly told me I must come down at once and take a peek at the shop. She sounded so excited that I hurriedly put my embroidery away and followed her. Pink! Pink, my love, and a pink like you had never imagined. An explosion of pink. Dark pink on the outside, but nothing too audacious or frivolous, nothing that made our house look indecent in any manner. A simple, elegant sign above the door: "Flowers. Orders for all occasions." The window arrangements were adorable, as pretty as a picture, trinkets and flowers, a profusion of good taste and feminity, the perfect way to catch a coquette's eye or a gallant gentleman in search of a becoming boutonnière. And inside, my dear, pink wallpaper, the latest rage! It looked magnificent. And so enticing.

I knew nothing about flowers, and neither did you, and Madame Colléville's humdrum taste certainly had not taught us anything. The shop brimmed over with flowers, the loveliest flowers I had ever seen: divine roses of the most unbelievable hues, magenta, crimson, gold, ivory; gorgeous peonies with heavy, droopy heads, and the smell in that place, my love, the intoxicating, dreamy perfume that lingered there, velvety and pure, like a silken caress.

I stood, entranced, my hands clasped. Like a little girl. Once again she glanced at me, unsmiling, but I caught a twinkle in those astute eyes. And then it seemed to me that her lips were quivering with amusement.

"So my landlady approves of the pink?" she murmured, rearranging bouquets with quick, deft fingers.

"It is lovely, mademoiselle . . . Lovely pink," I mumbled.

I did not know how to treat this haughty, prickly young lady. I felt shy in her presence, at first.

It was not until a full week later that Germaine came into the drawing room with a card for me. Pink, of course. And the most delicate scent emanated from it. *Would Madame Rose care to drop in for a cup of tea? AW.* And that is how our wonderful friendship started, nearly a decade ago. Over a cup of tea and roses.

I sleep not too badly down here. But even on the good nights, the same dream awakens me. It is a brief but hellish moment, when I am brought back to an agonizing instant I still cannot bring myself to voice and that you know nothing about.

I have been prey to this precise nightmare for the past thirty years. I must lie very still, wait for my beating heart to calm down. Sometimes I feel so weak that I need to reach for a glass of water. My mouth is parched and dry. This nightmare happened in your day, whilst I slept by your side, but I always managed to hide it from you.

Year after year, the same images come back, relentless. It is difficult to describe them without the fear sliding back to me. I see the hands prying the shutters open, the silhouette slithering in, the crack of the stairs. He is in the house. Oh, Lord, he is in the house. And the scream wells up inside of me, monstrous.

Back to the day the letter came, last year. Alexandrine wanted to know of my intentions. She bombarded me with questions as I sat quietly in my chair, my embroidery in my lap.

"But where are you going to go?" she asked worriedly. "To your daughter's? That is certainly the wisest move. When do you envisage your departure? Can I be of any help?"

I went on embroidering, calmly, trying not to let her guess the turmoil within me, the flutter of my heart. She put her hand on my arm, forcing me to look at her. Yes, she was that kind of person, you see, she demanded full attention.

"Madame Rose, I will surely find another position along the new boulevard, I am not afraid. It could take a while, as I am not as young as all that, getting on for thirty, am I not, and husbandless to boot!"

I had to smile at that. I knew she had enough energy within her to start all over, husband or no husband. She sighed, plucking at a loose curl of hair.

"I'm so fed up of people asking why I have no husband," she muttered fiercely, lowering her voice so that Germaine could not hear from the next room. "Really, people should stop nagging about why I am not married. Being an old maid does not bother me in the least, I have my flowers, and I have you, Madame Rose."

I listened to her, as I always did. I had become accustomed to her shrill voice. I rather liked it. When she stopped talking at last, I told her quietly I had no intention of moving. She gasped.

"No," I went on, impervious to her rising agitation, "I am staying right here. In this house."

And thus I told her, Armand, about what this house meant to you. I explained you were born here, as your father was before you. And his father, too. I told her this house was nearly a hundred and fifty years old, and had seen several generations of Bazelets. No one else but the Bazelet family had lived between these walls built in 1715, when the rue Childebert was created.

These past years, Alexandrine has often

asked about you and I have shown her the two photographs I possess and that never leave me. The one of you on your deathbed, and the last one of you and me a couple of years before your passing away, taken by the photographer on the rue Taranne. In that one, you have your hand on my shoulder, you look terribly solemn, I am wearing a coatdress and sitting in front of you.

She knows you were tall and well built, with chestnut hair, and dark eyes, and powerful hands. I have told her how charming you were, how gentle yet strong, how your soft laugh filled me with delight. I have told her how you used to write little poems for me, how you would slip them beneath my pillow, or in my ribbons and brooches, and how I treasured them. I have told her about your fidelity, your honesty, and that I had never heard you utter a lie. I have told her about your illness, how it came upon us and how gradually it took its hold, like an insect eating away at a flower, ever so slowly.

That evening, I told her for the first time how the house gave you hope during those last, difficult years. Being in the house was the only way to help you feel sheltered. You could not envisage leaving it even for an instant. And now, a decade after your death, I perceive that the house holds the same allurement over me. Do you understand, I tell her, do you see now that these very walls mean so much more to me than a sum I am to be given by the Préfecture?

And, as ever, whenever I mention the Prefect's name, I give full vent to my withering contempt. Tearing up the Ile de la Cité, heedlessly destroying six churches in the process, ripping apart the Latin Quarter, all for those straight lines, those endless, monotonous boulevards, all the same, high, butter-colored buildings, identical, a ghastly combination of vulgarity and shallow luxury. The luxury and emptiness that the Emperor wallows in and that I abhor.

Alexandrine rose to the bait, of course, as she always did. How could I not see that the great works being done to our city were necessary? The Prefect and the Emperor had imagined a clean and modern town, with proper sewers, and public lighting, and germ-free water, how could I not see that, how could I not agree with progress, with cleanliness, sanitary matters, no more cholera. (At that very word, oh, my dearest, I flinched, but said nothing, my heart fluttering . . .) She went on and on, the new hospitals, the new train stations, a new opera being built, the city halls, the parks, and the annexation of the districts, how could I be blind to all that? How many times did she use the word "new"?

I stopped listening to her after a moment, and she finally took her leave, as irritated as I was.

"You are too young to understand how I feel about this house," I said on the threshold. I could tell she wanted to say something, for she bit her lip and thus prevented herself from uttering a single word. But I knew what it was. I could hear her unspoken sentence floating in the air. *And you are too old.*

She was right, of course. I am too old. But not too old to give up the fight. Not too old to fight back.

The loud noises outside have stopped for the moment. I can creep around safely. But the men will soon be back. My hands tremble as I handle the coal, the water. I feel fragile this morning, Armand. I know I do not have much time. I am afraid. Not afraid of the end, my love. Afraid of all I need to tell you in this letter. I have waited too long. I have been cowardly. I despise myself for it.

As I write this to you in our icy, empty house, my breath streams out of my nostrils like smoke. The quill on the paper makes a delicate scraping sound. The black ink gleams. I see my hand, its leathered, puckered skin. The wedding ring on my left hand that you put there and that I have never taken off. The movement of my wrist. The loops of each letter. Time seems to slip by, endless, yet I am aware that each minute, each second, is counted.

Where do I begin, Armand? How do I start? What do you remember? Toward the end, you did not recognize my face. Docteur Nonant had said not to fret, that this meant nothing, but it was a slow agony, for you, beloved, and also for me. That gentle look of surprise whenever you heard my voice — "Who is that woman?" I heard you mumble, over and over again, gesturing toward me as I sat stiff-backed near the bed, and Germaine holding your dinner tray would look away, crimson-faced.

When I think of you, I will not drag that gradual decline back to me. I want to think about the happy days. The days when this house was full of life, love and light. Those days when we were still young, in body and in spirit. When our city had not been tampered with.

I am colder than ever. What will happen if I catch a chill? If I fall ill? I am careful as I move about the room. No one must see me. Lord knows who is outside, lurking. As I sip the hot beverage, I think of the fateful day the Emperor met the Prefect, for the first time. 1849. Yes, it was that year. That same terrible year, my love. A year of horror for us two, for other reasons. No, I shall not linger on that precise year at present. But I shall return to it when I feel I have mustered enough courage.

I read a while ago, in the newspaper, that the Emperor and the Prefect met for the first time in one of the presidential palaces, and I cannot help but think what an interesting contrast they must have made. The Prefect and his towering, imposing stature, those wide shoulders, that bearded chin and those piercing blue eyes. The Emperor, pale and sickly, his slight figure, his dark hair, his mustache barring his upper lip. I read that a map of Paris took up an entire wall with blue, green and yellow lines cutting through the streets like arteries. A necessary progress, we were all informed.

It was nearly twenty years ago that the embellishments of our city were imagined, thought out, planned out. The Emperor and his dream of a new city, modeled, you had pointed out over your newspaper, on London and its large avenues. You and I had never been to London. We did not know what the Emperor meant. You and I loved our city as it was. We were Parisians, both of us. Born and bred. You drew your first breath on the rue Childebert, and I, eight years later, on the nearby rue Sainte-Marguerite. We rarely traveled, rarely left the city, rarely left our area. The Luxembourg Gardens were our kingdom.

Seven years ago, Alexandrine and I, and most of our neighbors, walked all the way, over the river, to the place de la Madeleine, for the opening of the new boulevard Malesherbes. You had been gone for three years. You cannot imagine the pomp and ceremony of that event. I believe it would have made you very angry. It was a broiling summer day, full of dust, and the crowd was immense. People were sweating under their finery. For hours we were pushed and crushed against the Imperial Guard lining the premises. I longed to go home, but Alexandrine whispered to me that this was an important scene to witness, as a Parisian.

The Emperor arrived at last in his carriage. Such a puny man, I noted, and even from afar his skin had a yellowish, unhealthy hue. This was not the first time I laid eyes on our Emperor, as you will recall. Remember those flower-strewn streets after his coup d'état? Meanwhile, the Prefect awaited patiently in an enormous tent under the merciless sun. This was not the first time I had seen him either. He too, like the Emperor, was fond of parading, of having his portrait printed in every single newspaper. After eight solid years of demolitions, we all knew, as Parisians, exactly what our Prefect looked like. Or the Baron, as you preferred to call him. Despite the grueling heat, endless self-congratulatory speeches were given. The two men bowed to each other over and over again, and other men were called to the tent and made to feel most important. The oversized curtain masking the opening of the new boulevard swung open majestically. The audience cheered and clapped. But not I.

I already knew, then and there, that that tall bearded man with the redoubtable chin was to become my bitterest enemy.

I became so carried away writing all this to you that I did not hear Gilbert's knock. His is a coded one, two fast blows and one long scratch with the end of his hook. I do not believe you ever laid eyes on this particular fellow, although I recall you did enjoy conversing with a couple of ragpickers by the marketplace in the days when our daughter was small. I get up to unlock the door for him, ever so carefully, lest we should be seen. It is past noon now and the men will soon be back with the thunderous noises of their murderous enterprise. The door creaks, as it always does, as it has since the first day I set foot in this house, with you, all those years ago.

He is frightening to behold, at first. Tall, emaciated, blackened with grime and soot, his hair a tangled mess, his face a flurry of gnarled lines like the bark of a withered tree. The yellow of rare teeth, the green gleam of his eyes. He slips in, and brings his stench in with him, but I am accustomed to it now, an odd comforting mixture of eau de vie, tobacco and sweat. His long black overcoat is in tatters and sweeps the floor. His back is straight, despite the heavy wicker basket strapped to it. I know he stores all his treasures in there, all the bits and pieces he carefully scavenges in the streets at dawn, lantern in one hand, hook in the other: string, old ribbons, coins, metal, copper, cigar stumps, the rinds of fruits and vegetables, pins, strands of papers, dried-out flowers. And food, of course. As well as water.

I have learned not to turn up my nose at what he brings me. We share a hasty meal we eat with our fingers. No, not very daintily. Only one meal a day. As the winter deepens, it is less easy to find the coal to heat our frugal feast. I wonder where he gets the food, how he brings it back to me in our area that must now resemble a war terrain. When I ask him, he never answers. Sometimes I give him a few coins, from the little velvet purse I keep on me at all times, preciously, and which holds everything I own.

Gilbert's hands are dirty but exceptionally elegant, like a pianist's, with long tapered fingers. He never talks about himself, his past, how he has ended up on the streets. I have no idea how old he is. Lord knows where he sleeps, or for how long he has been leading this life. I met him five or six years ago. I believe he lives near the Montparnasse barrier, where ragpickers camp in a no-man's-land of shanty huts, and they make their way daily down to the Saint-Sulpice market through the Luxembourg Gardens.

I first noticed him because of his height and his strange top hat, obviously discarded by a gentleman, a battered and pockmarked affair, balancing on the summit of his head like a wounded bat. He had stretched out his vast palm for a sou, throwing me a toothless grin and a flash of those green eyes. There was something friendly and respectful about him, which was a surprise, as those lads can be surly and rude, as you know. His polite benevolence appealed to me. So I gave him a few coins, and walked home.

The next day, lo and behold, there he was in my very street, at the water fountain. He must have followed me. He was holding a red carnation, one that had probably tumbled out of a buttonhole.

"For you, madame," he said solemnly.

And as he walked toward me, I noticed his peculiar gait, his stiff right leg dragging behind him, giving him the clumsy stance of an outlandish dancer. "With the humble and devoted compliments of Gilbert, your servant."

With that, he swept off his hat, revealing his curly tangle of hair, and bowed down to the ground, just as if I had been the Empress herself.

He is the only person I talk to these days. It is a time of isolation and strife, and I thought I would find it more rigorous. My pampered life as your wife and widow, as a gentlewoman of the faubourg Saint-Germain, with a maid and a cook living under my roof, did not make this new existence all the more arduous. Perhaps I had been expecting it. I am not afraid of the discomfort, the cold, the dirt.

The only thing I am afraid of is not having enough time to tell you what I need to reveal. Not having enough time to explain. Let me try. Listen. The truth is that I love you, and that whilst you were slipping away, I could not tell you. I could not voice either my love or my untold secrets. Your illness prevented this. Little by little, over the years, you changed into a sick old man. It did not happen overnight, it was a slow process. But toward the end, you had no patience. You did not want to hear. You were in another world. Sometimes your mind was startlingly clear, especially in the mornings, and you once again became the real Armand, the one I missed and longed for. But it never lasted. The confusion in your brain took over again, relentlessly, and I would lose touch with you yet again.

This has no importance, Armand. I know you are listening to me now. You are all ears.

Gilbert, who has been resting by the heat of the enamel cooker, interrupts my writing to tell me about the destructions in the neighborhood. The magnificent Hôtel Belfort on our street is down. There is nothing left, he says. He watched it all. It did not take very long. A swarm of men, armed with their pickaxes. I listen, horror-struck. Madame Paccard has gone to live in Sens with her sister. She will never come back to Paris again. She left last fall, when we understood there was nothing to be done. Gilbert continues. The rue Childebert is empty at present, he tells me. Everyone has gone. It is a chilly ghost land. I cannot imagine our animated little street in that way. I tell Gilbert that the first time I set foot in this house was to buy flowers from Madame Colléville. This was nigh on forty years. I was nineteen years old. This seems to amuse him. He wishes to hear more.

I remember it was a spring day. In May. One of those fresh, golden mornings, full of promise. Mother wanted lily of the valley on a whim. She sent me to the rue Childebert flower shop, as she did not like the look of the white buds wilting in the market baskets.

Since I was a child, I had always reveled in the small, shady streets surrounding the church. They were peaceful and quiet compared to the loud bustle of the place Gozlin, where I lived. My brother and I had often taken strolls in this neighborhood, not far from our abode. There was less traffic here, hardly any carriages. People would line up at the Erfurth water fountain, nodding to each other politely. Children would play happily, watched over by their governesses. Shop owners had endless conversations on their doorsteps. Sometimes a priest in his long black robe, a Bible tucked under his arm, would be seen hurrying to the nearby church. On summer days, when the doors of the church were left open, hymns and prayers could be heard all the way down the street.

When I walked into the flower shop, I saw I was not alone. A gentleman stood there, a tall, strong man with a fine face and dark hair. He was wearing a blue tailcoat, and knee breeches. He was buying lily of the valley as well. I awaited my turn. And he suddenly offered me a budding stem. There was a shy expression in his dark eyes.

I found my cheeks to be burning. Yes, I was a coy creature. When I had turned fourteen, or fifteen, I noticed men looking at me in the streets, their gazes lingering upon me longer than necessary. At first it embarrassed me. I felt like crossing my arms over my chest and shielding my face under my bonnet. But it dawned upon me that this was what happened to girls as they became women. A young man that I had often met at the market with my mother had become enamored of me. He was a heavyset, red-faced boy who did not appeal to me. My mother found it amusing, and she teased me about him. She was a flamboyant chatterbox and I often hid behind her noisiness.

Gilbert smirks at all this. I think he is enjoying my tale. I tell him how the tall, dark man kept looking at me again and again. That day I was wearing an ivory dress with an embroidered collar, leg-of-mutton sleeves, a frilly bonnet and a shawl. Simple, but pretty. And yes, I suppose I was pleasant to look at, I tell Gilbert. A trim-waisted figure (which I have kept, despite the years), thick honey-colored hair, pink cheeks.

I wondered why the gentleman was not leaving the shop and why he was holding back. He waited till I had placed my order, and then as I stepped outside he prevented the door from closing as I passed. He followed me out to the street.

"Forgive me, mademoiselle," he murmured. "I do hope you will visit the shop again."

He had a low deep voice that I immediately found beautiful. I did not know what to say. I merely stared at the lily of the valley.

"I live just here," he went on, pointing to the row of windows above us. "This house belongs to my family."

He said this with a simple pride. I glanced up at the pale stone façade. It was an old, tall, square building with a slate tile roof, standing on the corner of the rue Childebert and the rue Erfurth, just by the fountain. There was a certain majesty about it. I counted three floors and each had four windows with gray shutters and iron-wrought railings, except for the two dormer windows up on the roof. The door behind the gentleman was painted dark green. Above the door knocker in the shape of a woman's hand holding a small globe, I read the name "Bazelet." (I did not know it then, no, I had no idea at all, but that name, and that house, would one day be mine.)

My family, he had said. Did he have a wife, did he have any children? I could feel my face redden. Why was I asking myself such intimate questions about this man? Those intent, dark irises made my heart beat faster. His eyes never left my face. So this was where this charming man lived, with his "family." Behind those smooth stone walls, behind that green door. Then I noticed a woman standing at the open window on the first floor, looking down at us as we stood in the street clutching our flowers. She was old, dressed in brown, her face weary and lined, but there was a pleasant smile floating on her lips.

"That's Maman Odette," said the gentleman, with the same gentle contentment. I looked at him closely for the first time. He was about five or six years older than me, perhaps more, and there was youth still in his face and stance. So he lived here with his mother. And he had not mentioned a wife, nor children. I saw no wedding band on his finger.

"My name is Armand Bazelet," he murmured, bowing elegantly. "I believe you live

in the neighborhood, I have seen you before."

Again I remained tongue-tied. I nodded,
cheeks pinker than ever.

"Near the place Gozlin, I believe," he went
on.

I managed to nod and to say:

"Yes, I live there with my parents and my
brother."

He beamed.

"Please do tell me your name, mademoiselle." He gazed at me beseechingly. I nearly
smiled at his expression.

"My name is Rose."

His face lit up and he promptly disappeared back into the shop. A couple of
minutes later, there he was, flourishing a
white rose.

"A beautiful rose for a beautiful young
lady."

I pause. Gilbert eggs me on. I tell him that
when I got home, my mother wanted to
know who had given me that flower.

"The transfixed suitor from the market,
perhaps?" she asked with a sneer.

I replied, very calmly, that it was Monsieur
Armand Bazelet of the rue Childebert and
she pursed her lips.

"The Bazelet family? The property owners?"

But I had not answered her and I went to my room overlooking the noisy place Gozlin, cradling the rose against my cheeks and lips, reveling in its velvety texture and delicious perfume.

And that is how you came into my life, my love, my Armand.

I have a treasure down here with me. An absolute treasure that I would never part with. What is it? you may well ask. My favorite frock? The lavender and gray silk one that you admired so? No, not any of my beloved dresses. I do admit, however, that it was agonizing parting with my clothes. I had recently discovered the most enchanting dressmaker on the rue de l'Abbaye, Madame Jaquemelle, a delightful lady with such an eye. Ordering from her was a treat. As I watched Germaine carefully fold away my clothes, I was struck by the fragility of our existences. Our everyday belongings are but mere nothings, carried away on a whirlwind of indifference. There they lay, packed away by Germaine, my dresses, skirts, shawls, cardigans, jackets, bonnets, hats, undergarments, stockings, gloves, off to Violette's house, to await me there. All the clothes that I would never lay eyes on again and that had been chosen with such infinite devotion (oh, the exquisite hesitation between two colors, two cuts, two materials). Those clothes had meant the world to me. And now they did not matter. How speedily we change. How quickly we evolve, as fast as a weather vane as soon as the wind turns. Yes, your Rose gave up her cherished garments. I can almost hear your gasp of disbelief.

So what is it, pray, that I hoard down here with me in a battered shoe box? You are longing to know, are you not? Well, letters! Precious, precious letters. A dozen of them or so, letters that mean more to me than outfits. Your first love letters to me. Yes, I have kept them preciously, for all those years. From Maman Odette. From Violette. From . . . I will not say his name. I cannot . . . From my brother, from the Baronne de Vresse, from Madame Paccard, from Alexandrine.

You see, they are all here, within arm's reach. Sometimes I merely place my hand on the box and it is a comforting gesture that soothes me. At other times I pull one out and read it, ever so slowly, as if it were for the first time. How intimate a letter is! The slant of a familiar handwriting has the same power as that of a voice. The scent which rises from the paper makes my heart beat faster. So you see, Armand, I am not really alone, as down here I have all of you right by my side.

Gilbert has left now, he will not be back till tomorrow morning, I presume. Sometimes he returns at nightfall to make sure all is well. The alarming noises have taken up again and I am writing this in the shelter he has built for me, in the cellar of Alexandrine's shop, through the little back door that opens up from our pantry into her boutique. This is where she used to stock her flowers, as Madame Colléville did before her. It is surprisingly warm down here. And much cozier than you would think. At first I was afraid the lack of windows would stifle me, but I soon became accustomed to it. Gilbert has made me a makeshift bed, comfortable enough, with the feather mattress that used to be in Violette's room, and a mound of very warm woolen blankets.

Down here the crashes and bangs are muffled and less worrying. It seems they grow closer and closer each day. I heard from Gilbert they started with the rue Saint-Marthe and the passage Saint-Benoît where I used to stroll with my brother, where you played as a boy. The pickaxes began their grisly business right there. I have not seen it, but I can all too well imagine the damage. Your childhood neighborhood has been destroyed, oh, my sweet love. Gone is the quaint coffee shop you used to go to in the mornings. Gone is the crooked passageway that leads to the rue Saint-Benoît, that dark, musty little alley with uneven cobblestones, where a friendly tabby cat used to frolic. Gone, the pink geraniums in the windows, gone, the cheerful children running along the street, all gone.

I feel safe down here in the hidden recesses of our house, with the flickering flame of the candle throwing tall shadows on the dusty walls around me. The occasional mouse scurries by. When I am nestling here, I lose track of time, of the day passing. The house holds me in its protective clasp. I usually wait till the crashes have abated. Then I creep up again to stretch my cramped limbs once all is silent.

How could I ever leave this house, beloved? This tall, square house is my life.

Every room tells a story. My story. Yours. I need to get those stories down on these leaves of paper, it is a terrible and unquenchable urge. I want to write all the stories out so that the words stand strong with a life of their own, so that they truly exist. So that the story of this house and its inhabitants will remain forever. So that we will not be forgotten. Yes, we the Bazelets of the rue Childebert. We lived here, and despite the snares that destiny threw our way, we were happy here. And no one, mark my words, no one can ever take that away from us.

Remember the first bellow of the water carriers just after dawn, coming to us as we lay upstairs in bed still, slowly emerging from sleep? The sturdy fellows would traipse down our street and across to the rue des Ciseaux, a tired donkey laden with barrels in their wake. Remember the regular swish of the street sweepers' brooms and the early morning peal of the church, so near it seemed the bell rang in our very room, and how nearby Saint-Sulpice would chime back like an echo, in harmony? The beginning of a new day, on our little street. The morning walk to the market with Germaine, when the cobblestones were still fresh, when cesspools had been emptied overnight, the little trot down the rue Sainte-Marguerite, shops opening one by one with the clang of metal shutters, down the rue Montfaucon and into the huge square of the market building, full of enticing smells and feasts for the eyes. I used to take Violette with me when she was a girl, as my mother had taken me with her, in her day. I took the little one too, twice a week. (I cannot face writing about the little one at present. Forgive me. Lord! What a coward I am.) You and I were born and raised between the black spire of Saint-Germain and the towers of Saint-Sulpice. We know this vicinity like the back of our hand. We know how the acrid tang of the river can linger through the rue des Saints-Pères when the heat of the summer is strong. We know how the Luxembourg Gardens flaunt a glittering coat of frost in the winter season. We know how the traffic becomes dense along the rue Saint-Dominique and the rue Taranne, when elegant ladies set out in hackneys sporting their coats of arms, when cabby drivers tussle with overburdened market carts and impatient, crowded omnibuses. Only riders on their horses manage to pick their way through the throng. Remember the rhythm of our young days, a pace that did not alter as I became a wife, a mother, and then your widow? Despite the upheavals that several times overtook our city due to political crisis and uproar, the business of living our life, the everyday preoccupation of cooking, cleaning, looking after the house, never wavered. When Maman Odette was still with us, remember how particular she was about the flavor of her bouillabaisse or the quality of her snails, even if angry mobs were parading down the streets? And the fuss with her laundry, how perfectly starched it had to be. Remember the end of the day? Dinner at six. The streetlights were illuminated one by one by the whistling lamplighter. On winter nights, we settled by the chimney. Germaine handed me a chamomile tisane and you sometimes savored a drop of liqueur. How tranquil, how calm those evenings were. The gleam from the lamp trembled ever so slightly, diffusing an appeasing rosy glow. You were most concentrated on your game of dominoes and then your reading. I, with my embroidery. The only noise to be heard was the crackling of the flames and your labored breath. I miss those undisturbed nightfalls, Armand. As dark deepened, and as the fire slowly petered out, we would retire. Germaine would have slipped the customary hot water bottle into our bed. And each evening heedlessly mingled into morning.

How well I see our sitting room in my mind's eye. It is but an empty shell now, stripped and bare like a monk's cell, but I still see it like it was. This was the first room

I set foot in when I came to meet your mother. Spacious and high-ceilinged, with emerald-green leaf-pattern wallpaper, a pale stone fireplace. Thick bronze-tinted damask curtains. Four large windows with colored panes, gold, crimson and violet, facing out to the rue Childebert. From there was a view down to the Erfurth fountain, where all our neighbors came for their daily supply of water. Fine woodwork, a delicate chandelier, crystal doorknobs, refined engravings of hunting scenes and countryside, lush carpets. An exotic cactus plant filled an alcove. On the large mantelpiece, a Roman marble bust of a young man, an ormolu clock with an enamel dial and a pair of gleaming silver candlesticks under glass shades.

That first day with your mother, when I came to visit her in the afternoon, I imagined you growing up here, as your father had before you. Your father died when you were fifteen, mine did when I was two, in a riding accident. I do not recall mine, and you did not often mention yours.

"My husband was impetuous and short-tempered," whispered Maman Odette over the coffee tray. "But Armand is such a patient son. His is a gentler, sweeter nature."

I know your mother accepted me from the

start, from the very day you introduced me to her. She was wearing a russet velvet dress with a high, heart-shaped bodice and flared sleeves, sitting in her favorite armchair, the large green one with the fringes, her knitting in her lap. She smiled at me with such kindness that it warmed my heart.

"So you have a brother, dear? What is his name?"

"Émile," I answered, as you handed me a slice of brioche on a pretty plate. Your eyes never left my face. And your mother looked on, glowing with happiness, her plump fingers working at her knitting.

She became a second mother to me in a mere couple of months, even before we married at Saint-Germain. My own mother, Berthe, had remarried when I was seven, a brash, loutish man, Edouard Vaudin. My brother Émile and I detested him. What a forlorn childhood we led on the place Gozlin. Berthe and Edouard lived only for themselves. We held no interest for them. Maman Odette gave me that most inestimable of gifts: she made me feel loved. Your mother treated me like her own daughter. For hours we would sit in the sitting room each time I came to visit, and I would listen with rapture to her tales, her talk of you and your youth, and how appreciative she was of you, her only son. She described the toddler you once were, the bright scholar, the loyal son, putting up with Jules Bazelet and his tantrums.

The first time you kissed me was in the stairway, near the creaking step, on our way up or down, I cannot recall, but I do remember that first kiss and the mad leap of my heart. For a man of your age, eight full years older than me, you were bashful. But I rather liked that. It soothed me.

When I came to visit your mother and you, in the very beginning, it was as if the rue Childebert welcomed me as soon as I walked up the rue des Ciseaux to the rue Erfurth and glimpsed the church's flank ahead of me. It was distressing to have to return to place Gozlin. Your mother's affection and your strengthening love drew a protective bubble around me. My mother shared nothing with me. She was too preoccupied with the vacuity of her life, the dinner parties she attended, the shape of her new hat, the twist of a new chignon. Émile and I had learned to fend for ourselves. We became friendly with the shopkeepers and café owners of the rue du Four while we waited for our mother to come home. The "petits Cadoux," we were known as, and we were offered hot pastry straight from the bakery oven, caramels and tidbits. The Cadoux children, well behaved and meek, in awe of their loud-spoken step-father.

I did not know what "family" meant until I met you and Maman Odette. Until the tall square house with the green door on the corner of the rue Childebert became my home. My haven.

Rue Childebert, June 12th, 1828

Dearest love, Rose of my heart,

This morning I walked down to the river and I sat on the banks for a while and enjoyed the morning sun. I watched the barges puff by, and the clouds surge through the sky, and I felt such a lucky man. A lucky man to be loved by you. I do not believe my parents loved each other at all, I think my mother put up with my father as best as she could, in a courageous, unselfish fashion that no one ever noticed because she barely complained.

When I think of next week, of when you will be mine, of that holy moment, I am overcome with joy. I cannot quite believe that you, the beautiful Rose Cadoux, will become my lawfully wedded wife. I have been to the church at Saint-Germain very many times, I was baptized there, I have attended mass, weddings, christenings, funeral services, I know the church inside out, I know it by heart, but now, in a mere couple of days, I will be walking you out of that church as if for the first time, with you, my wife, on my arm on that glorious day, on the blessed day that I will become your devoted husband. I will take you to the house on the rue Childebert where I was born, I will sweep you through that green door, up those stairs, up to our bedroom, and I will show you how much I adore you.

I have waited for you all my life, Rose. There is not only your regal beauty, your distinction, there is also and above all your altruism, your kindness. And your humor. I am entranced by your personality, your laugh, your adoration of pretty clothes, the way you walk, the gold of your hair, the fragrance of your skin. Yes, I am deeply in love. I have never loved like this. I was ready for a dutiful wife, a wife who would look after me and my household. You are so much more than an ordinary wife, because you are anything but ordinary.

This house on the rue Childebert will be our family home, sweet Rose. I am to be the father of your children. Our children will grow up in this neighborhood like I did, as you did. I want to see them come into their own, with you. I want the years to slip by peacefully, me at your side, within these walls. I am writing this to you in the living room which will soon become yours. This house will be yours too. Everything in it will be yours. This house will be a household of love.

You are loved, Rose, so deeply. You are young still, but such maturity emanates from you. You know how to listen. You know how to care. Oh, your eyes and their quiet beauty, their quiet strength.

I never want to be deprived of those eyes, that smile, that hair. Soon you will be mine, in name and in body. I am counting the days, and my ardent love for you burns through me like a bright flame.

Yours forever,
Armand

When I think of the sitting room, I cannot erase certain images from my head. There are happy ones, of course. Coming up the stairs as your bride, the lace soft on my face and neck, your hand warm at the small of my back. The murmur of the guests, but I only had eyes for you, my husband. In the cool obscurity of Saint-Germain I had murmured my vows, too timid to even glance up at your face, embarrassed by the crowd behind us, my mother and her fancy friends, her gaudy dress, her rakish hat.

I see myself as that young girl in white, still clasping the small bouquet of pale roses, standing in front of the fireplace, a new gold band tight on her finger. A married woman. Madame Armand Bazelet. The room could hold at least fifty people. Champagne and delicacies. But it seemed that you and I were alone. From time to time, your eyes would meet mine and I felt safe, safer than I had ever been in all my life, safe in your love, safe in your house. For I adored the house from the start, like I adored your mother. The house embraced me as your mother did. It took me in. I reveled in its particular smell, a mixture of beeswax and fresh linen, and good, simple cooking.

But there are not only fond, serene memories in this house. Alas. Some of those souvenirs are too difficult to bring back just now. Yes, I am fainthearted, Armand. My courage is coming to me in dribs and drabs. Please be patient. Let us start with this.

Remember the day we came back from a trip to Versailles with Maman Odette before Violette was born, and we found the front door had been forced? We ran up the stairs and discovered all our objects, our books, our clothes, our goods, piled up in a heap. The furniture had been overturned. The kitchen was a downright mess. Muddy footprints maculated the corridors and carpets. Maman Odette's gold bracelet had gone. So had my emerald ring and your platinum cuff links. And your secret cache of money near the chimney had been emptied. The police arrived, and I believe a couple of men searched the neighborhood, but we never got our things back. I remember how upset you were. You had another lock put on the door, a sturdier one.

Another very bleak remembrance. The sitting room brings back your mother. The day I met her, but also the day she died. Eight years span those two moments, the happy one and the dreadful one. Yet now, you see, as I write this more than thirty years later, they seem very close in time.

Violette was five years old, a little monster. Maman Odette was the only person who could tame her. Violette never had tantrums in front of Maman Odette. I wonder what magic her grandmother wrought. Perhaps it was simply authority that I lacked. Maybe I was too gentle a mother. Too lax. Yet I felt no natural inclination toward Violette. It was the little boy who later stole my heart. I put up with my daughter's temper, inherited from her paternal grandfather.

You were away that day, meeting the family notary near the rue de Rivoli. You would not be back till later that evening, for supper. Violette was sulking, as usual, her face screwed up in an unbecoming scowl. Nothing could possibly amuse her that morning, not her new doll or an enticing piece of chocolate. There was Maman Odette in her green-fringed chair, doing her best to glean a smile from her only grandchild. How patient and firm she was. As I bent over my sewing, I thought I should model my maternal initiatives on her calm, unyielding, yet tender manner. How did she do it? Experience, I presumed. Years of dealing with a mercurial husband.

I recall the clicking of the silver thimble against my needle, and Maman Odette's quiet hum as she caressed my daughter's hair. The hiss of the flames in the chimney. Outside, the rare clatter of a carriage, the patter of footsteps. A frosty winter morning. The streets would be slippery for Violette's walk, after her nap. I would have to hold her hand tight, and she hated that. I was twenty-seven years old and I led a comfortable, placid life. You were a kind, tender husband, a little absentminded sometimes, and you seemed strangely to age faster than I did. At thirty-five, you looked older than your age. Your distractedness did not bother me, I even found it charming, you sometimes forgot where your keys were, or what day it was, but your mother always pointed out you had already pronounced that very sentence, or that you had already asked that question.

I darned a tired sock, riveted to my task. Maman Odette had stopped humming. It was the sudden silence that made me raise my eyes to my daughter's face. She was gazing at her grandmother and she seemed fascinated, tilting her head as if to have a better look. I could only see Maman Odette's back as she leaned toward the child, her rounded shoulders in the gray velvet dress, her ample waist. Violette's eyes were dark with curiosity. What could her grandmother be telling her, what could her expression be, was she making a comical grimace? I laughed lightly and put the sock aside.

Suddenly Maman Odette let out a chortle, a horrible whistling sound, as if a morsel of food were stuck deep in her throat. I noticed with fright that her body was slowly sliding toward Violette, who had not budged, a tiny, petrified statue. I dashed forward as fast as I could to grab Maman Odette's arm and as her face swiveled around to me, I nearly fainted with horror. It was unrecognizable, colorless, her eyes two quivering white orbs. Her mouth gaped open, a glistening thread of drool dangling from her lower lip, and she choked again, just once, her plump hands fluttering to her bosom, helpless. Then she fell at my feet in a tumbled lump. I stood there, stunned, unable to move. I put my fingers to my chest, felt my heart pound.

She was dead. I could tell by merely looking at her, her immobile body, her chalky face, those hideous eyes. Violette rushed up and came to hide in my skirts, grasping at my thighs through the thick material. I longed to push her pinching fingers aside, to call for help, but I found I could not move. I simply stood there, thunderstruck. It took me a full minute or so to regain my strength. I ran to the kitchen, startling the maid. Violette had begun to wail in anguish. Long thin howls that hurt my ears. I prayed for her to be quiet.

Maman Odette was dead. And you were not at home. The maid shrieked when she discovered the body on the carpet. Somehow I mustered enough strength to order her to pull herself together and to fetch help. She fled, sobbing. I remained with the screaming child, unable to look at the body any longer. Maman Odette had seemed perfectly well at breakfast that morning. She had eaten her bread roll with appetite. Why had this happened? How could this be possible? She could not be dead. The doctor would come, he would resuscitate her. Tears began to trickle down my cheeks.

At last the old doctor came lumbering up the stairs carrying his black bag. He wheezed as he crouched down on his knees to press two fingers to Maman Odette's neck. Then he wheezed even more as he laid his ancient ear on her bosom. I waited and prayed. But he shook his grizzled head. And then he closed Maman Odette's eyes. It was over. She was gone.

When my father died, I was only a child and did not remember. Maman Odette was the first of my beloved to go. Her death loomed over me. How would I cope without her smile, the sound of her voice, her whims, her mellow laugh? Objects around our home reminded me constantly of her, as if to taunt me. Her fans. Her bonnets. Her collection of tiny ivory animals. Her gloves that bore her initials. Her Bible, which never left her reticule. The small pouches of lavender that she tucked away here and there, their enchanting fragrance.

The sitting room slowly darkened with people. The priest who married us arrived and endeavored to comfort me, in vain. The neighbors began to gather in front of the house. Madame Colléville was in tears. Everyone was fond of Maman Odette.

"It was her heart, no doubt," the old doctor informed me as Maman Odette's body was carried to her room. "Where is your husband?"

They all asked where you were, again and again. Someone offered to have a message sent to you at once. I believe it was Madame Paccard, of the Hôtel Belfort. I rummaged around your bureau to find the notary's address. And then, as I stroked my daughter's head, I could not help thinking of that messenger of ill bearings making its way over to you, steadily, edging closer and closer. You did not know. You sat with Maitre Regnier, going over bequeathals and investments, and you had no idea. Wincing, I imagined the look in your eyes when you were handed the slip of paper, the way your face would blanch when the words made sense, the stagger to get to your feet, your greatcoat thrown over your shoulders, your top hat askew, your cane left behind in your haste. Then the way home over the river, in a hackney that seemed to crawl at a snail's pace, the traffic dense, the roads icy, and the horrid thud of your heart.

Your face as you came in. I shall never forget it.

"Where is she?" you said, looking at me, stooping to embrace our stricken daughter.

"Upstairs," I murmured, feeling faint.

You flung your coat at me, loosened your cravat. Your gestures were awkward, almost brutal.

"What happened, Rose?"

I saw your eyes were brimming with tears.

I clasped your hand in mine, feeling your trembling pain. I told you, simply, how your mother had died. The tears ran down your cheeks in silence. Then you squared your shoulders, and you went up the stairs to see your mother's body, alone. I stood at the bottom of the stairs with your coat in my arms and I wept.

She meant the world to you, as she did to me. She was our pillar of strength, our source of wisdom. We were her children. She cared for us so tenderly. Who would care for us now?

The hideous day dragged on, burdened with the aftermath of death and its demands. Condolences pouring in, flowers, cards, whispers, murmurs, mourning clothes and their disheartening darkness. Our front door draped with black, passersby crossing themselves.

I felt the house sheltering me, holding me strong within its stone walls like a sturdy ship during a tempest. The house nursed me, soothed me. You were taken up by paperwork and the preparation of her burial at the Cimetière du Sud, where your father and grandparents lay. The mass was to be held at Saint-Germain. I watched your intent agitation. Violette was unusually silent, clasping her doll to her chest. People

84

moved around us in a never-ending ballet of purposefulness. From time to time an affectionate hand would pat my arm or offer me a beverage.

Again Maman Odette's white face floated back to me. The choking, whistling sound. Had she suffered? Could I have prevented this? The memories resurfaced. Our daily walks to the market, then across to the rue Beurrière, over to the Cour du Dragon where she enjoyed looking at the workshops and talking to the blacksmith. Her unhurried trot, her arm tucked under mine, the bob of her bonnet at my shoulder. When we reached the rue Taranne she liked to pause for a while, her cheeks pink, her breath short. She would lift her brown eyes to me, so like yours, beaming up at me. "What a pretty girl you are, my Rose." My mother never once told me I was pretty.

Rue Childebert, September 28th, 1834
My very dear Rose,

How empty the house is without you, Armand and the little girl! My, my, it seems so big all of a sudden, the very walls echo my loneliness. Two long weeks until you all come back from your trip to Burgundy. How on earth am I going to manage? I cannot bear sitting in the living room alone. My knitting, my newspaper, my Bible, everything falls from my hand. I realize now, in these grim moments, how much you mean to me, my sweet Rose. Yes, you are the daughter I never had. And I sense that I am closer to you than your mother is, bless her heart. How lucky we are to have found each other through my son, your husband. You are the light of our lives, Rose. Before you came to live here, a certain gloominess lurked within these walls. It was you who brought the laughter, the cheerfulness within.

I believe that you have no idea of all this. You are such an unselfish, pure person, Rose. Yet beneath that sweetness there is a very great strength. I sometimes wonder what you will be like when you are my age. I cannot for the life of me envisage you as an old lady, as you are youth embodied. The graceful swing of your step, the gold richness of your hair, your smile and those eyes. Oh, yes, my Rose, those eyes. They will never fade. When you are old and gray as I am now, your eyes will blaze on, so blue.

Why have you turned up so late in my existence? I know I will not live very many more years, the doctor has warned me about my heart, and nothing much can be done about my state. I go for my little walks without you, and they are much less pleasurable. (Madame Collévillé accompanies me and she walks terribly slowly and smells of something sour that is displeasing . . .)

Yesterday we witnessed a fight on the rue de l'Echaudé. It was marvelously dramatic. Some fellow had had too much, no doubt, of the Green Fairy and was bothering a finely dressed lady. Another man told him to stop it, shoved him away from the lady and then the drunkard lunged forward, there was a dreadful crack, a shriek, blood, and the poor man who had tried to save the lady got his nose broken. At that point yet another man joined into the battle, and soon, before you could draw breath, the entire street was full of wrestling, sweating men. The lady stood there, clutching her parasol and looking perfectly lovely and silly. (Oh, you would have adored the way she was dressed, I recall it especially just for you: one of those hourglass-shaped dresses, a blue-spotted delight, and a rather dashing bonnet with an ostrich feather that trembled as much as she did.)

Come home soon, dearest Rose, and bring my loved ones home safely as well.

Your doting mother-in-law,

Odette Bazelet

I did not sleep well last night. The nightmare tormented me once more. The intruder, making his way up the stairs slowly, taking his time, fully aware that I am upstairs, asleep. The creak of the stairs, how well I hear it and how it fills me with dread. I know that bringing back the past is never a peaceful process. It awakens turmoil and regret. Nevertheless, the past is all I have left. I am alone now, my love. Violette and my pompous son-in-law believe I am on my way to them. My grandchildren are expecting their grandmère. Germaine is wondering where Madame is. My furniture arrived last week, my valises and trunks were delivered a few days ago. Germaine has probably unpacked all my clothes, my room in their large home overlooking the Loire is no doubt ready. Flowers by the bed. Fresh sheets. When they will become worried, they will surely write. I do not feel much concern.

Nearly fifteen years ago, when the Prefect started his massive destructions, we learned that my brother Émile's lodgings were to be torn down for the opening of the new boulevard de Sébastopol. Émile had not seemed concerned, he was to be paid a good sum in compensation, and with his wife Edith and their children, they had decided to move to the west of the city, where her family dwelled. Émile was not like you, not attached to houses. For you, houses are like people, are they not, they have a soul, a heart, they live and breathe. Houses remember. Émile is now an elderly gentleman with gout and no hair, and I believe you would not recognize him. I find he resembles my mother, thankfully he does not possess her vanity and her emptiness. Merely the longish nose and dimpled chin that I did not inherit.

After our mother passed away, just after the coup d'état, and after Émile's house had been razed, we did not see much of him, did we? We had not even been to visit their new place in Vaucresson. But you were fond of my brother, of "Mimile," as we used to call him affectionately. He became the little brother you never had.

One inauspicious afternoon you and I had

90

decided to walk over to the renovations to look at the progress. Émile had already moved into his new abode with his family. You ambled slowly then, Armand, your illness was taking its toll, you only had two more years to live, which of course we knew nothing about. You could still stroll quietly at my side, holding on to my arm.

We were unprepared for what awaited us. Our peaceful faubourg Saint-Germain had nothing to do with what we saw. This was no longer Paris. This was war.

We simply did not know where we were anymore. We had walked up the rue Saint-André-des-Arts, expecting to end up on the rue Poupée, as usual, but the latter had vanished.

In its place gaped a gigantic pit hemmed in by buildings in ruins. We looked around us in a daze. Where on earth was Émile's old house? Émile's neighborhood? The restaurant on the rue des Deux Portes where we celebrated his wedding? The renowned bakery on the rue Percée? And that pleasant boutique where I had purchased those fashionable embroidered gloves for Maman Odette? There was nothing left. We inched along, stupefied.

We discovered that the rue de la Harpe had been savagely truncated. The rue Serpente as well. All around us, crumbling edifices seemed to quiver perilously, bearing shreds of wallpaper, charred and blackened passages of fireplaces, doors absurdly still hanging on hinges, intact flights of stairs spiraling into nothingness. It was a hallucinatory sight and bringing it back now still makes me nauseous.

We gingerly picked our way to a more sheltered spot, looking down with anguish to the heart of the pit. Hordes of workers carrying pickaxes, shovels, hammers, swarmed like a gigantic army through mounds of rubble and billowing clouds that stung our eyes. Thick streams of horses pulled planks on carts. Here and there bonfires burned furiously with unimaginable rage, as men loaded more timber and more debris into the voracious flames.

The noise was abominable. You know, I can still hear the harsh crackle of the blaze, the shouts and the yells from the workers, the unbearable hammering of pickaxes digging into the stone, the deafening thuds that made the earth under our feet shudder. Our clothes were soon mottled by a thick layer of soot, our shoes coated with lime, and the hem of my dress was sodden. Our faces were gray with grit, our mouths and tongues parched. We both coughed and puffed, tears streaming down our faces. I could feel your arm shaking next to mine. I noticed that we were not the only spectators. Other people had gathered to watch the destructions. Their grimy faces were awed, their eyes red and watery, smarting from the ashes and the dust.

We had read about this in the newspaper — we knew, like all Parisians, that parts of our city were to be renovated — but never had we imagined this inferno. And yet, I mused, transfixed by what I was seeing, this was where people had lived and breathed, this had been their home. Over there, on that disintegrating wall, was the vestige of someone's fireplace, with the faint trace of a painting that used to hang there. A family had gathered in front of that mantelpiece in the winter. And that cheerful wallpaper used to line another person's bedroom, somebody had slept and dreamed here, and now what was left? A wasteland.

Living in Paris under the reign of our Emperor and our Prefect was like living in a besieged city invaded daily by dirt, rubble, ashes and mud. Our clothes, shoes and hats were always dusty. Our eyes always stung, our hair was perpetually thick with a fine gray powder. How ironic, I thought as I patted your arm, that right next to this massive field of ruins other Parisians placidly got on with their lives. This was only the beginning, and we were not aware of what lay ahead. We had been putting up with the embellishments for three or four years. Little did we know then that the Prefect would not relent, that he would inflict the inhuman pace of expropriations and demolitions on our city for fifteen more years.

We decided hastily to take our leave. You were deathly pale and your breath was short. How could we ever get back to the rue Childebert? We had lost our bearings. We were in unknown territory. Wherever we turned, panicked, we were met with pandemonium, blizzards of ashes, thunderlike explosions, avalanches of bricks. Mud and soggy waste churned under our feet as we desperately tried to find our way out. "Get away, for God's sake!" boomed a furious voice as an entire façade collapsed only a short distance away with an earsplitting crash and the piercing smattering of broken glass.

We took hours reaching home. That evening you did not speak. When we sat down to dinner, you ate nothing and your hands trembled. I began to understand that bringing you to see the destructions was a terrible mistake.

I tried to comfort you, I repeated the very words you had uttered when the Prefect was appointed:

"They will never touch the church, the houses around it, we are safe, our house is safe."

You would not listen to me. You left the table and went to the window, clasping and unclasping your hands. I watched you slowly scratch the side of your face over and over again, to such an extent that I longed to pry your nails from running down your cheeks.

"Come and have some warm soup, dearest," I begged, "it will do you good after that long walk."

Your eyes were glassy and wide, and I knew you kept seeing the façades crumbling, the swarms of workers hacking away at the buildings and the flames blazing in the pit.

I got up to try to coerce you back to the table, but you pushed me away, quite savagely. I did not know what to do. So I sat there, helpless, immobile, till the food became cold and it was cleared away in silence. Getting you to come to bed that night was also an ordeal. Again you shoved me away, wordlessly, with a new vehemence that shocked me.

It was in those moments, I believe, that the first signs of your illness became most apparent. I had not noticed these signs before, but now they were obvious. Your mind was undergoing a sort of confusion. You were agitated, distracted, you seemed lost.

It was from then on that you refused to leave the house, even for a short walk to the gardens. You remained in the sitting room, your back upright, facing the door. You would sit like that for hours, heedless of me, of Germaine, of anyone speaking to you. You were the man of the house, you muttered, yes, that was exactly what you were, the man of the house. No one was going to touch your house. No one.

After your death, the destructions went on, led by the merciless Prefect and his bloodthirsty team, but in other parts of the city. I was too intent on learning how to survive without you.

But two years ago, well before the letter arrived, an incident took place. And then I knew. Yes, I knew.

It happened as I was leaving Madame Godfin's shop with my chamomile tisane. I noticed a gentleman standing on the street corner in front of the water fountain. He was painstakingly setting up a camera, and a deferential assistant was hovering nearby. It was early, I recall, and the street was not yet busy. The man was short and sturdy, with graying hair and a mustache. I had not seen very many cameras before, only at the photographer's on the rue Taranne who had taken our portraits.

I slowed down as I approached him and watched him at work. It seemed a most complicated affair. At first I could not comprehend what he was photographing, as there was no one in sight apart from me. His apparatus was facing the rue des Ciseaux. As he fiddled about, I discreetly asked the young assistant what their business was.

"Monsieur Marville is the Prefect's professional photographer," announced the young man, his chest fairly bloating with pride.

"I see . . ." I answered. "And who is it that Monsieur Marville will be photographing at present?"

The young fellow looked down at me as if I had said something incredibly stupid. He had an oafish face and bad teeth for his age.

"Well, madame, he does not photograph people. He photographs streets." Another swell of his torso. "According to the Prefect's orders, and with my help, Monsieur Marville is photographing the streets of

Paris that are to be destroyed for the renovations."

Vaucresson, April 26th, 1857

My dear sister,

  We are now installed in our new abode, in Vaucresson. I believe it would take you a mere couple of hours to get to us, should you and Armand care to drop by, which I very much hope you will. But I understand that your eventual visit will have to do with your husband's strength. The last time I saw him, he had already much declined. I am writing this to tell you, dear sister, how unfair I find your situation. For the past years, you and Armand have struck me as being a profoundly happy couple. Such happiness is rare, I find. You recall, no doubt, our miserable childhood, the threadbare affection our mother (bless her soul) bestowed upon us. I believe I do not share with my wife anything quite as deep and meaningful as what you share with your husband. Yes, life has been cruel with you, and I still cannot bring myself to write my nephew's name. But despite the blows that fate has dealt you, Armand and you have always seemed to rise above those blows and I admire that tremendously.

I think you would like this new house, Rose. It stands on a hill, and has a long, green garden which the children enjoy. It is large, and sunny, and most cheerful. It is far from the noise and dust of the city, far from the Prefect's works. I sometimes think Armand would be happier in a place like this than in the dark rue Childebert. He would revel in the sweet perfume of grass, the nearby woods, the song of the birds, but then, of course, I remember how both of you love your neighborhood. Odd, isn't it? Whilst I grew up, with you, in place Gozlin, I already cherished the fact that one day I was going to leave. Even if Edith and I lived a long while on the doomed rue Poupée, I fully knew that I would not end my days in the city. When we received the letter from the Préfecture informing us that our house was to be destroyed, I realized that this was the change I had always been waiting for.

I know you believe the rue Childbert is safe, Rose, because it is so near the church at Saint-Germain. I know how much Armand's family home means to him. But don't you believe that attaching such importance to a house is unwise? In his state of mind, losing his abode would be an utter disaster. Do you not think that it would be more judicious to move away from the city? I could help you find a charming place near us, here in Vaucresson. I think you would appreciate the calm and harmony of this little village. You are not yet fifty, there is still time to move on and start again, and you know that Edith and I would help. Violette is happily married, living in Tours, raising her children, she does not need her parents anymore. There is nothing to hold you back in Paris.

I beseech you, Rose, do think this over. Think of your husband's health and of your well-being.

Your affectionate brother,
Émile

It is a sweet relief being certain that no living soul will ever set eyes on what I have been scribbling away at, down here. I feel liberated, and my confessions, although a burden, appear slightly alleviated. Are you with me, Armand? Can you hear me? I like to think you are right here, by my side. I do wish I possessed a camera, like Monsieur Marville, and that I could have photographed every single room of our house in order to immortalize it.

I would have started with our bedroom. The heart of our house. The other day, when the movers came to pack up our furniture to send it to Violette's place, I spent a long moment in our bedroom. If walls could speak, would they not have related so many tales? They have witnessed death and life. I stood where the bed was, facing the window, and I said to myself, This is where you were born, this is where you died. This is where your father passed away, and probably his father as well. This is where I brought our children into the world.

I would always remember the canary-yellow wallpaper, the bordeaux velvet drapes, the arrowheaded curtain rods. The marble fireplace. The oval mirror with its gilded frame. The graceful bonheur du jour, its drawers full of letters, stamps and pens. The small table inlaid with rosewood where you put your spectacles, your gloves, and where I stacked the books purchased from Monsieur Zamaretti's shop. The wide mahogany bed with brass fittings, and your gray felt slippers by the left side, where you used to sleep. Yes, I will always remember how the sun shone here, even on a winter morning, running a triumphant golden finger along the walls, lighting the yellow to an incandescent gold.

When I think of our room, the acute pain of childbirth comes back to me. They say women forget with the passing of time, but no, I shall never consign to oblivion the day Violette was born. My mother had not spoken to me about the matters of life before I got married. But then, what did my mother speak to me about? Search as I might, I cannot recall an interesting conversation, a memorable moment. Your own mother had murmured a few words before my confinement for our first child. She had said to be brave. The words sent a chill down my spine. The obstetrician was a placid gentleman who never spoke much and the midwife who came to visit me was always in a hurry, as there was another lady in the neighborhood who needed her assistance. I had started the pregnancy well enough, with hardly any queasiness or other disorders. I was twenty-two years old, and healthy.

The scorching heat of July. It had not rained for weeks. My labor had already commenced and the ache in my back gradually grew more and more pronounced. I suddenly wondered if what was lying ahead for me would not be utterly dreadful. I dared not complain for the moment. I lay on the bed, Maman Odette patting my hand. The midwife arrived late. She had been caught up in a mob and turned up breathless, her bonnet tied crookedly. We had no idea of what was happening outside. She informed you and Maman Odette in a low whisper that people were starting to manifest, that it was getting ugly. She thought I could not hear, but I did.

As the hours ticked by and as I began to comprehend with rising anguish what Maman Odette had meant when she had said to "be brave," it became clear that our child had chosen to make its entrance into the world in the midst of a seething revolution. From our small street, we could hear the growing grumble of insurrection. It started with shouts and cries, and the clatter of hooves. You were told by panic-stricken neighbors that the royal family had fled.

I heard all this from far away. A damp cloth was held to my forehead, but it neither eased the pain nor lessened the heat. Sometimes I retched, my insides churning in agony, bringing up nothing but bile. In tears, I confessed to Maman Odette that I was not going to be able to carry this ordeal through. She tried to pacify me, but I could tell she was anxious. She kept going to the window and peering outside. She went down to talk to you and to the neighbors. The riots were everyone's priority, not this baby. Nobody cared, it seemed, about this baby and me. What would happen if you all left the house, even the midwife, if you all had to go and to leave me here, helpless, unable to move? Did all women go through this horror, or was it only me? Had my mother felt this, did Maman Odette when she had you? Unthinkable questions that I never dared voice and that I can only write now because I know no one will read this.

I recall that I began to sob uncontrollably, pain and terror ripping my stomach apart. As I lay twisting with pain in a bed drenched with sweat, I could hear yells of "Down with the Bourbons!" coming in through the open window. The deep boom of cannonballs startled us, and the midwife kept crossing herself nervously. The sharp rattle of gunshots was heard not far off and I prayed for the baby to come, I prayed for the insurrection to end. I did not care in the least for the fate of our King, of what was going to happen to our city. How selfish I was, thinking only of myself, not even of this baby, only of me and the monumental pain.

It lasted for hours, night sliding into day, and the constant agony tearing me open with prongs of fire. You had discreetly slipped away, you were no doubt downstairs in the sitting room with Maman Odette, and I did everything I could to keep my gasps silent within me, at first. But soon the excruciating waves took over again, higher and higher, and I had to let the screams out, trying to muffle them behind my moist palm or a pillow, but soon nearly delirious with pain, I gave full vent to the shrieks, heedless of the open window and of you, sitting below. Never had I screamed so loudly, so strongly, in my entire life. My throat was parched. No more tears came. I thought I was going to die. And at moments, when it became unbearable, I even wanted to die.

It was when Notre Dame's loudest and deepest bell boomed out in warning, in a never-ending litany that penetrated my exhausted brain like a sledgehammer, that the baby was born at last, during the worst of the riots, the last of the three bloody days, whilst the Hôtel de Ville was stormed. Maman Odette was told that the tricolor flag of the people flew high over the rooftops and that the white and gold flag of the Bourbons was nowhere to be seen. You heard there had been many civilian deaths. A little girl. I was too drained to be disappointed. She was put to my breast and as I peered down at her, a shriveled, grimacing creature, I inexplicably felt no surge of love, nor pride. She pushed me away with tiny fists and a mewing of complaint. No, it was not love at first sight between me and my daughter. And thirty-eight years later, nothing has changed. I do not know why this happened. I cannot explain. It is a mystery to me. Why does one love a child, and not another? Why does a child push a mother away? Whose fault is it? Why does it happen so early, at birth? Why can nothing be done about it?

I felt her resentment grow, year after year. Do you remember, a couple of years after Maman Odette's death, that scene in the dining room? Violette was still a child, and already so brittle. I cannot recall how the argument sparked off, where it came from. She had been complaining, as usual, and I had reprimanded her.

"Try to see the bright side, darling, you are persistently negative," I said smoothly, with a warm smile.

Oh, how she scowled at me.

"When I grow up," she spat, "I want to be nothing like you, Maman. You are too pretty, too good, too nice. I want others to respect me."

I remember you rebuked her, with your customary mildness, however. She remained silent for the rest of the meal, but her words had wounded me, deeply. Too pretty, too good, too nice. Was that how my own daughter, a mere girl, considered me? A mealymouthed, spineless belle?

She has become a hard woman, all bones and angles, not an ounce of your gentleness, or my kindness. How is it that we can bear children of our flesh and blood and yet feel no link to them, so that they seem like strangers? She looks like you, I presume, your dark eyes and hair, your nose. She is not pretty, but she could have been, had she smiled more. She does not even possess my mother's petulance, her coquettish vanity that was sometimes amusing. What does my son-in-law, the prim and proper Laurent, see in her? A perfect housewife, I imagine. She is a good cook, I believe. She runs that country doctor's household with a hand of steel. And her children . . . Clémence and Léon . . . I know them so little . . . I have not laid eyes on their sweet faces for years . . .

That is my only regret now, dearest. As a grandmother, I would have liked to bond with my offspring. It is too late. Perhaps being a disappointed daughter turns one into an inadequate mother. Maybe the lack of love between Violette and me is my fault. Maybe I am to blame. I imagine you patting my arm with that *tut, tut* expression of yours. But you see, Armand, I did love the little boy so much more. You see, it is conceivably my doing. Now, in the winter of my life, I can look back and state these facts, almost without pain. But not without remorse.

Oh, my dear, how I miss you. I look down at the last photograph I have of you, the one of your deathbed. They had dressed you in your elegant black suit, the one you wore for best occasions. Your hair, hardly touched by gray, was swept back, and your mustache had been groomed. Your hands folded on your chest. How many times have I looked at that photograph since you have gone? Thousands, I believe.

I have just had the most terrible fright, dearest. My hands are shaking so much I can barely write this. Whilst I was poring over each detail of your face, there came a loud rattle of the front door. Someone was trying to get in. I leaped up, my heart in my throat, knocking my cup of tea to the floor. It fell with a deafening clatter. I froze, horrorstruck. Would they hear it? Would they understand someone was still in the house? I crouched down very low, close to the wall, and made my way slowly to the entrance. There were voices out there, the shuffle of feet. The handle jounced again. I glued my ear to the panel, breathless. Men's voices, rising loud and clear in the frosty morning.

"This one is due to go soon, the work will start next week, most probably. The owners moved out, it's as empty as an old shell."

A shove against the door made the wood

jiggle against my face. I moved back quickly.

"The old door's mighty sturdy still," remarked another male voice.

"You know how fast those houses come down," sneered the first voice. "Won't take long to raze it, or the entire street, as it were."

"That's right, this little street and the one round the corner will be down in a jiffy."

Who could these men be? I wondered, as they at last drew away. I spied at them from a crack behind the shutters. Two youngish fellows in formal suits. Probably from the Prefect's team, in charge of the renovations and embellishments. Resentment surged through me. These people were heartless, no better than ghouls. They had no heart, no emotions. Did they even care that they were pulling people's lives to pieces by destroying their homes? No, they did not.

The Prefect and the Emperor dreamed of a modern city. A very great city. And we, the people of Paris, we were mere pawns in this huge game of chess. *Sorry, madame, your house is on the future boulevard Saint-Germain. You will have to move out.* How had all my neighbors gone through this? I mused, as I carefully picked up the pieces of the broken cup. Had it been easier for them? Had they collapsed in tears when

112

they had left their house, when they had turned around to look at it for the last time? That charming family just up our street, the Barous, where were they now? Madame Barou, like me, had been heartbroken at the idea of leaving the rue Childebert. She too had come here as a young bride, had given birth to her children in that house. Where were they all now? Where had they gone? Monsieur Zamaretti had come to bid me farewell, just before the order to evacuate the street. He had found another business on the rue du Four Saint-Germain, with a fellow bookstore. He kissed my hand in a most Italian-like fashion, bowing and scraping, promising to visit me in Tours, at Violette's place. Of course, we both knew we would not see each other again. But I shall never forget Octave Zamaretti. After you departed, he saved my life, as Alexandrine did. Saved my life? I can imagine you looking perfectly astonished. I will get around to that later, Armand. I have a good deal to tell you concerning Octave Zamaretti and Alexandrine Walcker. Bear with me, dearest.

Monsieur Jubert had vanished into thin air shortly after the expropriation decree had been issued. His printing house had a forlorn and neglected air about it. I wondered where he went. I wondered what happened to the dozen workers who came there every day to earn their living. I did not care much for Mademoiselle Vazembert and her crinoline, no doubt she found herself a protector, ladies with those kind of physiques do that with ease. But I already missed Madame Godfin and her stout figure, her smile of welcome as I came in to purchase my tisanes, the spick-and-span shop that smelled of herbs, spices and vanilla.

It is difficult to imagine that my little world, made of the familiar, everyday figures of our street, Alexandrine and her irresistible window displays, Monsieur Bougrelle and his pipe, Monsieur Helder greeting his customers, Monsieur Monthier and the enticing wafts of chocolate emanating from his boutique, Monsieur Horace's guttural laugh and constant invitations to sample his latest delivery, were all doomed to disappear. Our colorful street with its low buildings sheltering near the church was to be wiped off the face of the earth.

I knew precisely what the boulevard would look like. I had seen enough of what the Prefect and the Emperor had done to our city. Our tranquil neighborhood was to be flattened out so that the monstrous, noisy new artery could spring forth right here, just by the church. The enormous width of it. The traffic, the noise, the omnibuses, the throng.

In a hundred years' time, when human beings will be living in a modern world that no one can even fathom, not even the most adventurous of writers or painters, not even you, dearest, when you liked to imagine the future, the small, quiet streets branching out like a cloister from the church will be buried and forgotten, forever.

No one will remember the rue Childebert, the rue Erfurth, the rue Sainte-Marthe. No one will remember the Paris that you and I loved.

There is a sliver of glass down here, amidst the rubbish Alexandrine did not have time to throw out. I can see my face in it, if I tilt it in a certain fashion, taking care not to slice my fingertips. In age, my face has lost its ovalness, it has become longer, less graceful. You know I am not vain, yet I do take pride in my appearance, I have always been careful about my clothes, my shoes, my bonnets.

Even in these last, strange moments, I will not look like a ragpicker. I do my toilette as I can, with the water Gilbert brings me, and the perfume I keep at hand, the one the Baronne de Vresse gave me last year, when Alexandrine and I met her at her house on the rue Taranne to go shopping at the Bon Marché. I have heard the rue Taranne is safe, for the moment. But for how long? Will they dare destroy its splendor? Will the ravenous boulevard devour it as well? Swallow it up in one gulp?

I still have the same eyes, the ones you loved. Blue or green, depending on the weather. My hair is silver now, with the faintest trace of gold. I never thought of dyeing it, the way the Empress does, and that I find so vulgar.

Ten years is a long time, is it not, Armand? Writing this letter to you brings you remarkably close. I can almost feel you looking over my shoulder as I write this, your breath on my neck. I have not been to visit you at the cemetery for a long while. It is painful for me to see your grave, your name etched out on the stone, and Maman Odette's, but even more heart-wrenching is the name of our son, Baptiste, just below yours.

There, I have written his name for the first time in this letter. Baptiste Bazelet. Oh, the pain. The dreadful pain. I cannot let that pain in, Armand. I must fight against it. I cannot surrender to it. If I do, I will drown in it. If I do, I will have no strength left.

The day you died, you gathered up a last spark of lucidity. You said to me, upstairs, in our bedroom, my hand in yours: "Watch over our house, Rose. Don't let that Baron, that Emperor . . ." And then your eyes were coated over by that film of strangeness and you once again gazed at me as if you did not know me. But I had heard enough. I knew fully what you demanded of me. As you lay there, the life gone from your body, with Violette's sobs at my back, I was aware of the task you had left me. I was to honor it. I made you that promise. Ten years later, my dearest, and now that the time is coming, I have not wavered.

The very day you left us, the fourteenth day of January, we learned that a terrible attack had been planned on the Emperor near the old Opéra, on the rue Le Peletier. Three bombs were thrown, nearly two hundred people were wounded and a dozen died. Horses were torn to pieces, and all the windowpanes of the entire street were shattered. The royal carriage was turned upside down, and the Emperor narrowly escaped death, as did the Empress. I later read that her dress had been drenched with a victim's blood, but that she went to the Opéra all the same, in order to show her people that she was not afraid.

I did not care for that attack, as I did not care for the Italian who perpetrated it, Orsini (who was later to be guillotined), nor did I care about what his motives were. You were slipping away and absolutely nothing else mattered to me.

You died peacefully, with no pain, in our

room, in the mahogany bed. You seemed relieved to be leaving this world and all the things about it that you no longer understood. Over the past years, I had watched you gradually slip into the illness that lurked in the recesses of your mind and that doctors talked about prudently. Your disease could not be seen or measured. I do not even think it had a name. No medicine could ever cure it.

Toward the end, you could not stand the light of day. You had Germaine close the shutters of the sitting room as of noon. Sometimes you would jump in your seat, startling me, and you would cock an ear, straining, and you would say, "Did you hear that, Rose?" I had not heard a thing, be it a voice, a bark, the slam of a door, but I learned to say that, yes, I had heard it too. And when you began to say, agitated, over and over again, your hands twitching, that the Empress was coming over for tea, that we must have Germaine prepare fresh fruit, I also learned to nod my head and to soothingly murmur that all that was being done, of course. You liked to read the paper thoroughly, every morning, poring over it, even the advertisements. Every time the Prefect's name was printed, you let forth a stream of insults. Some of them were very rude.

The Armand that I miss is not the old, confused person you were at fifty-eight, when death overcame you. The Armand I long for is the strong young man in his knee breeches with the gentle smile. We were married for thirty years, dearest. I want to go back to those first days of passion, your hands on my body, the secret pleasure you gave me. No one will ever read these lines, so I can tell you how well you pleased me, and what an ardent husband you were. In that bedroom upstairs, you and I loved each other like a man and a woman should. But then, when the illness started to gnaw away at you, your loving touch relented and slowly withered away with the passing of time. I suspected I no longer sparked any desire. Was there another lady? My fears abated and a new anxiety dawned when I understood you no longer felt any desire, for another lady, or for me. You were ill, and desire had waned forever.

There was that abominable day, toward the end, when I was returning from the market with Mariette, and we came upon Germaine in tears in the street in front of the house. You had gone. She had found the sitting room empty, and your hat and cane had disappeared. How could this have happened? You hated leaving the house. You never did. We searched the area high and low. We went into every single shop, from Madame Paccard's hotel to Madame God-fin's boutique, but no one, from Monsieur Horace, who spends a lot of time loitering on his threshold, to anyone from the printing house having a pause, saw you that morning. There was no sign of you. I rushed to the commissariat near Saint-Thomas-d'Aquin and explained the situation. My husband, an elderly, confused gentleman, was missing, and had been so for the past three hours. I loathed having to describe your malady, having to tell them you had lost your head, that sometimes you were frightening, when your derangement took over. You often forgot your name, I told them, and therefore how would you ever make your way back home, if your address also escaped you? The commissaire was a kindhearted fellow. He asked for a precise description of you. He sent a dispatch out to look for you and told me not to worry. But I did.

In the afternoon a huge storm broke. Rain drummed over the roof with tremendous force and thunder boomed so hard the foundations shook. In anguish I thought of you. What were you doing now, had you found shelter somewhere, had somebody taken you in? Or had a loathsome stranger, making the most of your confusion, committed a heinous deed?

As the rain poured down, I stood by the window, with Germaine and Mariette crying behind me. I could bear it no longer. I went outside, my umbrella soon useless as the rain drenched me through and through. I managed to walk to the soggy gardens, spread out in front of me like a yellow sea of mud. I tried to envisage where you could have gone. To your mother's grave, to your son's? To the churches? To a café? The night was falling now, and still there was no sign of you. I staggered back home, stricken. Germaine had prepared a hot bath. The minutes ticked by, ever so slowly. You had now been gone for over twelve hours. The commissaire came by, his face grave. He had sent his men to all the nearest hospitals, to make sure you had not been taken there. In vain. He left, urging me to keep my spirits up. We sat by the table, facing the door, silent. The night wore on. We could not eat, nor drink. Mariette's nerves gave way and I sent her up to her room, as she could barely stand.

In the dead of the night came a knock on the front door. Germaine ran to open up. We saw an elegant young man wearing hunting habits and pantalets. There you were next to him, haggard but smiling, holding on to Père Levasque's arm.

"I had been hunting in the Fontainebleau forest with friends in the late afternoon and I came across this man who seemed lost," explained the young stranger, who introduced himself as Hector Bouteiller. "At first this gentleman had not been able to declare his identity, and he kept mentioning the church at Saint-Germain-des-Prés, so I drove him here in my hackney."

All the while you stood there, my dearest, a bewildered smile on your face. Germaine held her apron to her mouth, her cheeks ashen. Père Levasque added, sotto voce:

"They came to the church, Madame Rose, and I of course immediately recognized Monsieur Bazelet."

I asked everyone to step inside. You still had that dazed, benign expression on your face. I was thunderstruck. The forest was miles away. I had been there once as a child and it had taken the entire morning. How on earth had you ended up there? Who had taken you there, and how? I longed to ask you these questions.

I thanked the young man and Père Levasque profusely, offered them coffee and a liqueur and gently led you to our room. I understood that you had no answers to give me. I went to wake Mariette and we sat you down and examined you carefully. Your clothes were filthy, caked with mud and dirt. There were tufts of grass and thorns in your shoes. I noticed dark stains on your waistcoat. More worriedly, there was a deep gash on your throat and red scratches on your hands. Mariette suggested we call for young Docteur Nonant, even at this hour. I agreed. She wrapped her cloak around her and went out into the night to fetch him, with Germaine.

When the doctor at last arrived, you were falling asleep, your hand in mine, breathing peacefully, like a child. The doctor tended to you. I cried silent, hopeless tears of relief mingled with fear, clutching your fingers, going over the incomprehensible events of the day. We would never know what happened to you, how and why you had been found hours away from the city, wandering in the forest with a bloody throat. You would never tell us.

Although I had been prepared by the doctor concerning your oncoming death, it came to me as a dreadful blow when it happened. I was approaching fifty, and I felt my life was behind me forever. I was alone. At night I would lie awake in our bed and listen to the silence. I could no longer hear your breath, the rustle of the sheets as your body moved. Without you, our bed felt like a cold and humid tomb. It seemed to me that even the house silently asked where you were. Your armchair, cruelly empty. Your maps, your papers, your books, your pen and ink, and no longer you. Your place at the dinner table, screaming out your absence. The pink shell you had bought at the antique shop on the rue des Ciseaux and that sounded like the sea when you pressed it to your ear. What do we do when our loved ones leave us forever and we are left behind with the mundane objects of their everyday life? How do we cope? Your comb and hairbrush had me in tears. Your hats. Your game of chess. Your silver pocket watch.

Our daughter had moved to Tours, had been living there for the past eight years, she had two children. My own mother had passed away seven years ago, and my brother Émile had already left the city. The only people around me were our neighbors, and their companionship and support were treasures to me. They all pampered me. Monsieur Horace dropped off small bottles of strawberry liqueur, and Monsieur Monthier offered me mouth-watering chocolates. Madame Paccard invited me to lunch every Thursday at the hotel. Monsieur Helder, for an early dinner at Chez Paulette, on Mondays. Madame Barou visited me once a week. Père Levasque and I walked to the Luxembourg Gardens every Saturday morning. But there still was a gaping, aching hole in my life when you left me. You were a quiet man, yet you took up a vast amount of silent space and that was what I missed. Your sturdiness and strength.

I hear Gilbert's coded knock and get up to answer it. It is absolutely freezing this morning, and my skin is purple with cold. Gilbert limps in, clapping his gloved hands together and stamping on the floor. The icy blast he lets in has me shivering from head to toe. He heads straight for the enamel cooker and revives the coals with gusto.

I watch him. I tell him about the men from the Préfecture who tried to open the front door. He says gruffly:

"No need to worry, Madame Rose, there is no work this morning, too cold. We can have the heater going all day, no one will notice the smoke. The area is totally deserted. I'm pretty sure the work will be halted for a while."

I huddle near the heat, feeling it thaw the iciness that had engirdled my entire body. He heats bits of food on a greasy saucepan.

The appetizing smell tickles my nostrils, my stomach grumbles. Where does Gilbert get the coal, the food? Why is he doing this for me? When I ask him, gently, he merely smiles.

After our meal, he hands me a letter with a grin. He says the postman was hovering around, baffled, not knowing what to do with the mail, now that the street had been closed down and condemned. How he had managed to obtain my mail, I do not know. Gilbert is a mysterious fellow and he enjoys surprising me.

The letter, as I suspected, is from our daughter. It was written over a week ago.

Maman dear,

We are most alarmed by the fact that you have not yet arrived. Germaine is convinced that something has happened to you and I pray that she is wrong.

The last time I heard from you, you said you would be here by the beginning of the month. All your personal effects are here by now and your larger furniture is in storage.

Laurent has been told of a charming little house by the river, not far from us, and not too expensive, where we do think you would be perfectly comfortable. You will be pleased to know that it is not damp at all, he says. There is ample room for Germaine, of course. A pleasant elderly lady we are friendly with lives right next door. But if you prefer to stay with us, this is of course possible.

The children are well and are looking

forward to your stay with us. Clémence plays the piano beautifully and Léon is learning how to read. Please send word with more precise details concerning your arrival. We cannot understand where you are.

My husband is convinced that it is healthier for you to leave the faubourg Saint-Germain and to let yourself be looked after by us. At your age, nearly sixty after all, this is the right thing to do. You must not go on living in the past and letting grief overcome you.

We eagerly await your news.

Your daughter,

Violette

Even her handwriting makes me wince, it is so sharp and implacable. What to do? I must have looked puzzled because Gilbert asks me what was wrong. I explain who the letter is from and what Violette wants. He shrugs.

"Write back to her, Madame Rose. Tell her you are staying with friends. That you are taking your time coming down to her. Stall her."

"But how do I get this letter to her?" I ask.

Another careless shrug.

"I'll go post it for you, at the post office."

He smiles down at me paternally, flashing those ghastly teeth.

So I went to fetch a piece of paper and I sit and write the following letter to my daughter.

Dearest Violette,

I am indeed sorry for causing you and your husband to worry about me. I am staying for a while with my friend the Baronne de Vresse. I believe I have told you about her. She is a charming socialite that I met through Mademoiselle Walcker, my flower lady. Yes, she is very young, she could be my granddaughter, but she has taken a fancy to me. We enjoy each other's company.

She has most generously offered to put me up before I come down to you. She has a lovely house on the rue Taranne. As a result, I am not in the least involved in the destructions of our neighborhood which I am no witness of. We go shopping at the nearby Bon Marché and she takes me to Worth, the grand couturier where she has her dresses made. I am enjoying an enchanting stay, going to the theater, the opera and balls. An old lady of nearly sixty can still do these things, I assure you.

I will let you know when I arrive, but do not count on me for quite a while yet, as I plan to stay with the Baronne de Vresse as long as possible.

Do give my warmest regards to your husband and children, and to my dutiful Germaine. Tell her that Mariette has found a good position with a well-to-do family near the Parc Monceau.

Your affectionate mother

I cannot help smirking at the irony lurking in a couple of those sentences. Balls, theaters, Worth, indeed! No doubt my daughter, the typical humdrum provincial wife, would feel a twinge of envy reading about my dazzling fictitious social life.

I clear my throat and read the letter out loud to Gilbert. He grunts.

"Why don't you tell her the truth?" he asks abruptly.

"About what?" I say.

"About why you are not leaving this house."

I pause for a little while before I answer him.

"Because my daughter would not understand."

In my dreams, my good dreams, he comes back to haunt me, my little one. I see him tearing down the stairs, then his shoes clattering along the cobblestones outside. I hear his voice, his peals of laughter. The color blue suited him, and I had all his chemises made from different blues, and his jackets and his cardigans as well, even his cap was blue. My blue and gold prince. When he was a baby, he used to sit in my lap very quietly and observe the world around him. I suppose the first objects he ever detailed were the engravings in the sitting room, and the portraits above the mantel-piece. His round, curious eyes would go from corner to corner, taking it all in, his thumb in his mouth. He breathed peacefully against me. His little body felt warm against mine.

I felt such contentment in those moments. I felt I was truly a mother, a sensation I had never experienced with Violette, my first-born. Yes, this tiny being was mine, and mine to protect and cherish. They say mothers prefer their sons, is this not the secret truth? Are we not born to bring sons into the world? Yet I know you loved your daughter. She bonded with you in a way I never did.

When I dream of Baptiste, I see him napping, as a child, upstairs in the children's room. I marvel at the mother-of-pearl lids covering his eyes, lashes fluttering. The round smoothness of his cheeks. His parted lips, his slow, calm breath. I gazed at that child for hours, while Violette played with her friends downstairs, watched over by the nanny.

I did not like the nanny touching him when he was a baby. I knew it was not proper for me to spend so much time with him, but I could not help it. He was mine to feed, mine to cuddle. He was the center of my life, and you looked on benignly. You felt no jealousy, I think. Maman Odette had been that way with you. You were not surprised. I took him everywhere I could. If I had a hat to choose or a shawl to buy, he would be with me. All the shopkeepers knew our son. All the market vendors knew his name. He was never vain about his popularity. He never took advantage of it, either.

When I dream of him, as I have for the past twenty years, I awake with tears in my eyes. My heart aches. It was easier when you were there, as I could reach out into the dark and feel your comforting shoulder.

There is no one for me now. Just the cold and deathly quiet. I cry alone. I know how to do that, very well.

Bussy-le-Repos, July 6th, 1847

Petite Maman,

I am having a spendid time with Adèle and her family at Bussy. I miss you, Violette and Papa very much. But I am still having wonderful time. So dont worry. I miss home. Very nice here. And very hot. Yesterday we bathed in the pond. Not very deep and Adèle's big brother took me on his shoulders and was covered in mud. Adèle's mother makes escalopes. I eat so much sometimes my tummy hurts. I miss you in evenings when it is bedtime. Adèle's mother kisses me but shes not pretty like you she does not have soft skin Maman smell. Please write another letter why do letters take so long to arrive. Adèle's father not as funny as Papa. But hes still nice. He smokes a pipe puffs smoke into your face. Theres a big white dog I got scared of at first because he jumps at you but thats his way of saying hello. His name Prince. Can we have one too. And there is also a cat called Mélusine but she hisses at me so I don't stroke her. I am trying to write this best I can. Adèle's brother is correcting my mistakes he's a fine chap I want to be like him when I grow up hes ten years older than me. Adèle had a fit last night there was a spider in her bed awfully big one Maman please go look in my bed make sure there is no spider I miss you and love you and give my love to Papa and to my sister.

Baptiste Bazelet
Your son

I felt an icy hand on my bosom and I screamed through the silence. Of course, there was no one there, no icy hand, how could anyone ever find me down here, hidden in the cellar? I need a moment to quiet my heart, to breathe in a normal fashion. I can still hear the creak of the stairs, still see the large, freckled hand gliding up the banister, still sense the pause just outside my door before he enters. Will I ever be free? Will the terror ever leave me? The house no longer protects me, in that nightmare. The house has been invaded. It is no longer safe.

Wrapped up in several layers of thick woolen shawls, I take a candle up to the top floor, to the children's room. I have not been up there for a while, even when the house was still lived in. It is a long, low-ceilinged room with beams, and as I stand on the threshold, I can still see it filled with toys and games. I can still see our son, his golden curls, his sweet little face. I used to spend hours in this room with Baptiste, playing with him, singing songs to him, all those things I never did with my daughter, simply because she never let me.

As I let my eyes roam over the now-empty room, I remember the happy times with the little boy. You had decided get the house repaired, to mend all its various problems: leaks in the roof, various cracks, general wear and tear. Every nook and cranny was inspected. A team of workers came steadfastly, and the house was repainted, woodwork repaired, floors repolished. They were a cheerful, good-natured lot, and we grew to know them well. There was Monsieur Alphonse, the foreman, with his black beard and loud voice, and there was Ernest, his ginger-haired attendant. Groups of different workers came every week, hired for their specific skills. Every Monday you would note the progress and discuss various elements of it with the foreman. It took up a great deal of your time, and you were most earnest about the entire matter. You wanted the house to look its best. Your father and your grandfather had not done much to it, and you took it upon yourself to refurbish it.

Even while there was work being done in

the house, we had friends to stay, friends to dinner. I recall that it took up much of my time, those menus to work out, the seating of guests, and which room needed freshening for a new arrival. I took those tasks most seriously. Each menu was carefully written out in a special book so that I would never serve the same meal twice to my guests. How proud I was of our house, how cozy and pretty it looked on those winter evenings, with the fire blazing in the chimney, and the soft light of the lamps. Happy times.

Over that blessed decade, Violette turned into a silent, self-centered young girl. She was a good learner, and she was serious, but we shared so little. We had nothing in common, like my mother and I. She talked more with you, I believe, but she was not close to you either. As for Baptiste, she had little interest in him. There was a nine-year difference between her brother and her. She was like the moon, silvery, cold and distant, and he was a triumphant golden sun, all blaze, all fire.

Baptiste was a child touched by grace. His birth had been short and painless, which astounded me, as I had geared myself up for the ordeal I had endured with Violette. There he was, this splendid child, healthy, pink and energetic, his eyes already wide open to the world. How I wished Maman Odette could have seen her grandson, but she had already left us four years earlier. Yes, that decade was a golden one, as gold as our son's hair. He was a simple, happy child. He never complained, or if he did, he did it with such charm that he'd melt anyone's heart. He liked to build little houses with colored bricks made of wood that you gave him for his birthday. For hours he would carefully construct a house, room by room.

"That is your bedroom, Maman," he would proudly state. "And the sun shines in, just the way you like it. And Père will have a study right here, with a big desk so he can set all his papers down and do his important work."

This is so difficult to write, Armand. I fear the power of words, how they may wound you, like the stab of a knife. The candlelight flickers over the bare walls. I am afraid. Afraid of what I must say. Many times, during confession with Père Levasque, I tried to unburden myself. But it was impossible. I never did.

I feared the Lord would take my son, that my time with him was counted. Every moment with him was a delight. A delight tainted with fear. Another revolution had stormed our city in February. This time I was not bedridden, and I saw it all. I was forty years old, still sturdy, still strong, despite my years. The riots broke out in the poorer quarters of the city, and barricades went up, barring the streets with iron grillwork, overturned carriages, furniture, tree trunks. You explained that the King had failed to end political corruption, that the economic crisis that raged was without precedent. This had not concerned me, as my daily life as a mother and wife had not altered. It is true that the prices at the market had soared, but our meals were still abundant. Our life was still the same. For the moment.

1849. Baptiste was ten years old. The year the Prefect and the Emperor met for the first time. The year after the barricades and the February Revolution. Nearly twenty years ago, and my heart still bleeds as I write this. He moved like a little pixie always on the go, spry, fast as lightning. His laugh echoed through the house. Sometimes, you know, I still hear it.

There were early murmurs of the disease. I was first aware of them at the market. The last epidemic breakout was just after Violette was born, ten years before. Thousands of people had died. One had to be very careful with the water. Baptiste enjoyed playing at the fountain on the rue Erfurth. I could see him from the window, the governess watching over him. I had warned him, you did too, but he had a mind of his own.

It happened very fast. The papers were already full of the oncoming deaths, the toll was rising day after day. The dreadful word sent terror into our homes. Cholera. A lady on the rue de l'Echaudé had succumbed. Every morning a new death was announced. Fear gripped our street.

And then, one morning, in the kitchen, Baptiste collapsed. He fell to the floor with a shriek of pain, crying out that he had a cramp in his leg. I rushed to him.

"What is it, my darling, my sweet?" I murmured as he fretted, twisting and turning in my arms. Germaine suggested we pull up his breeches to see what was wrong with his leg. My fingers clumsily worked the buttons.

"Maman," muttered my son, "it hurts . . ." How I remember his thin, weak voice, a voice that tugged at my heart.

There appeared to be nothing wrong with his shin or thigh. I soothed him as best as I could. His forehead felt hot and clammy. He began to sob, wincing with pain. A horrid gurgle was heard, coming from his abdomen. I said to myself that this could not be happening. No, not to my son, not to my adored son. Not this. I remember screaming out for you, screaming your name up the stairs.

You heard my shriek and you rushed down, your face white as a sheet. Yes, I can still hear your footsteps pounding down the steps. You had a book in one hand, your spectacles clutched in the other. Violette followed in your wake, her eyes wide.

"Rose, what on earth . . . ?"

Then you saw our son and the objects clasped in your fingers clattered to the floor. Violette screamed. Remember how we carried him up to his room, you and I, and Germaine rushed to summon the doctor? But it was too late. I could tell by your face that you knew, but you were not telling me. In a mere couple of hours, hours that spelt doom and death with every click of the minutes gliding past, all liquids left his burning, twisting body. They poured out of him, oozed from him and we could only watch with horror.

"Do something!" I pleaded to the doctor. "You must save my son!"

All day long, young Docteur Nonant wrapped my son's loins in strips of clean sheets, slid clear water down his throat, but to no avail. Baptiste's hands and feet seemed to have been dipped in black paint. His pink little face, dry and waxen, had gone a monstrous bluish color. The round cheeks had caved in to leave in their wake the disturbing pointed mask of a wizened creature I no longer recognized. His sunken eyes cried no more tears. The sheets thickened with all he was bringing up, soiled rivulets that gushed from his body in a never-ending, stinking flux.

"We must all pray at present," murmured Père Levasque, whom you had sent for in the last, dreadful moments when we finally understood that there was no more hope. Candles were lit, and the fervent mutter of prayers filled the room.

When I look at the room now, that is what I remember: the stench, the candles and the prayers, over and over again, Germaine's gentle sobbing, Violette's cough. You sat very straight and silent by my side, and sometimes you took my hand and squeezed it gently. I was so beside myself with grief that I could not understand your calm. I remember thinking: Faced with the death of a child, are men stronger than women because they do not give birth, because they do not know what it means to carry life within one and to bring a baby into the world? Are mothers not linked to their offspring by a secret, intimate and physical link that fathers cannot experience?

That night, in that house, I saw my beloved son die and I felt my life become a meaningless void.

The year after, Violette married Laurent

Pesquet, her fiancé, and left home to live in Tours. Nothing touched me anymore since the little boy's death.

I watched the events of my life unfold from very far away. I went about my existence in a sort of dazed numbness. I remember you talking about me with Docteur Nonant. He had come to visit me. At forty-one, I was too old to have another child. And no other child could ever replace Baptiste.

But I knew why the Lord had reclaimed my child. I shake as I write this, and it is no longer the cold.

Forgive me.

Rue Childebert, August 20th, 1850
Rose of my heart,

I cannot bear your pain, your sorrow. He was the loveliest child, the most delightful boy, but alas God decided to call him back to Him and we must respect His choice, there is nothing else we can do, my love. I write this by the fireplace, as the candle flickers through the quiet night. You are upstairs, in our room, trying to find rest. I do not know how to help you and I feel useless. It is a loathsome feeling. I wish Maman Odette were here to console you. But she has been gone so long now, and she never knew the little boy. Yet she would have surrounded you with her love and her tenderness in these agonizing moments. Why are we men so hopeless at this sort of thing? Why do we not know how to soothe, how to bestow our care? I am furious with myself as I sit here and write this to you. I am but a worthless husband, as I cannot bring you solace.

Since he left us, last year, you are the ghost of your former self. You have become gaunt and white, you no longer smile. Even at our daughter's recent wedding, on that gorgeous day by the river, you did not smile once. Everyone noticed and of course everyone spoke to me about it, your brother, very worried, and even your mother, who never notices what state you are in, and your new son-in-law, a young doctor, had a quiet word with me about you. Some of them suggested a trip down south, by the sea, to seek the sun and warmth. Others said to rest, to eat nourishing food, to exercise.

Your eyes are empty and sad, it breaks my heart. Oh, what am I to do? Today I walked about our neighborhood and I tried to find you a trinket that would cheer you up. I came back empty-handed. I sat down at the café on the place Gozlin, near where you grew up, and read the newspapers, all full of Balzac's death. As you know, he is one of my favorite writers, and somehow, because of what you are enduring, your acute pain, I simply cannot feel sadness at Monsieur de Balzac's passing away. The poor fellow was more or less my age. And he too had a wife he loved passionately, as I love you with a passion that inflames my entire life.

Rose, my love, I am a wistful gardener who no longer knows how to make his lovely plant come into full, promising bloom. Rose, you are now frozen, as if you no longer dared to burst into flower, no longer dared to offer yourself to me, to let your enticing perfume bewitch me as those delicious petals open up one by one. Is the gardener to blame? Our beloved son is gone, and with him, a part of our life. But our love is still powerful, is it not, and it is our greatest strength, it is what we need to cherish in order to be able to survive. Remember how our love preceded our child, how our love gave birth to him. We must treasure it, nurture it and revel in it. I share your sorrow, I respect and mourn our son as a father, as a parent, but can we not mourn him as lovers? For after all, was he not born of two splendid lovers? I long for the sweet scent of your skin, my hands yearn to caress the curves of your beloved body, my lips burn to bestow thousands of kisses on the secret places that only I know of and adore. I want to feel you undulate against me under the softness of my caresses, under the sweet violence of my embrace; I hunger for your love, I want to taste the sweetness of your flesh, your womanly intimacy, I want to go back to the feverish ecstasy we shared as lovers, as a husband and a wife deeply, truly in love, up there in the quiet kingdom of our bedroom.

You are my priority, Rose, and I shall fight with all my might to restore your faith in our love, in our life.

Yours forever,

Armand, your husband

I felt the overpowering need to take a pause and could no longer write for a short while. But now, as my quill once more slides along the paper, I am connected with you again. I did not write you very many letters. We never separated, did we? I have also kept all your little poems. They are not really poems, are they? Little sentences of love that you would leave here and there for me to find. How I miss them. When the longing becomes too great, I give in, and reach for them. I keep them in a small leather pouch with your wedding ring and your reading glasses. "Rose, dear Rose, the light in your eyes is like the dawn, but only for me to behold." And this one: "Rose, enchanting Rose, no thorns on your stem, only buds of sweetness and love." No doubt a stranger would find them puerile. I do not care.

When I read them, I can still hear your lovely, deep voice. Armand, I miss your voice, above all. Why can't the dead come back and talk to us? You could whisper to me as I take my tea in the mornings, and you would murmur more words at night, when I lie awake in the silence. And I would like to hear Maman Odette's laugh, and my son's babble. My mother's voice? No, not in the least. I do not miss it whatsoever. When she died, of ripe old age, in her bed, at place Gozlin, I felt nothing, not even a twinge of sadness. You were standing beside me and Émile, and you kept looking at me, as if you read something on my face. I wanted to tell you that it was not my mother I missed, no, it was still yours, Maman Odette, who had died nearly twenty years before. I think you knew. And I was still mourning my son. For years after his death, I went to his grave every other day, walking all the way to the Cimetière du Sud, by the Montparnasse barrier. Sometimes you came with me. But most often I went alone.

A strange, painful peace invaded me when I sat by his tomb, under the rain, or the sun, my umbrella protecting me on every occasion. I did not wish to talk to anyone, and if someone hovered too near, I would swoop under the umbrella to safety and privacy. A lady of my age came to a nearby grave with the same regularity. She too would sit for hours, her hands in her lap. Was she praying? I wondered. I sometimes prayed. But I preferred to talk to my son directly. I talked to him in my head, exactly as if he had been standing in front of me. In the beginning, the presence of the other lady disturbed me. I soon got used to her. We never spoke to each other. Sometimes we nodded, very quickly. Who was she mourning? A husband, a son, a daughter, a mother? Did she talk to her dead the way I did?

You never asked what I said to Baptiste when I visited him. You were most respectful. I can tell you now. I gave him all the news and tidbits about our neighborhood. I told him how Madame Chanteloup's shop on the rue des Ciseaux nearly burned to the ground and how the firemen fought all night long to master the flames and how exciting yet horrible it had been. I told him how his friends were bearing up (funny little Gustave on the rue de la Petite Boucherie, and rebellious Adèle on the rue Sainte-Marthe). I told him how I had found a new cook, Mariette, talented and timid, and Germaine bossed her around in a scandalous fashion until I put my foot down, or rather you did, as the man of the house.

Day after day, month after month, year after year, I went to the graveyard to talk to my son. I told him things I never dared tell you, my very dear. Our new Emperor, for instance, and how I was not impressed by the runt of a man parading on his horse under a cold drizzle with crowds hollering, "Long live the Emperor!" especially after all those deaths during his coup d'état. I told him about the great balloon bearing a majestic eagle that floated over the roofs in the Emperor's wake. The balloon was rather impressive, I whispered to Baptiste, but the Emperor was anything but that. However, you believed, at that time, like the majority of people, that the Emperor was "remarkable." I was far too soft-spoken to voice my true political feelings. So I quietly told Baptiste that in my humble opinion, those haughty Bonapartes were far too full of themselves. I told him about the lavish wedding at the cathedral, with the new Spanish-born Empress that everyone wanted to see, that everyone made a fuss of. And then, when the Prince was born, I told him about the cannonballs fired from the Invalides. How jealous I was of that baby prince! I wonder if you ever felt it. Seven years beforehand, we had lost our own baby prince, our Baptiste. I could not bear reading the interminable articles in the press about the new royal child, and I carefully averted my eyes so that every new and sickening portrait of the Empress preening herself with her son could no longer be seen.

Gilbert has interrupted me with the most astounding news. He has just seen Alexandrine skulking along the street. I asked him what he meant. He looked at me sternly.

"Your flower girl, Madame Rose. The tall, dark one with all that hair and a round face."

"Yes, that's her," I said, smiling inwardly at his description, which was most fitting.

"Well, she was just outside the house, Madame Rose, peering in. I thought she was going to ring on your bell or open the door, so I gave her a little fright. It's getting mighty dark out there, and she nearly jumped out of her skin when I popped out of that corner. She scuttled off like a frantic hen, and she did not have time to recognize me, I can assure you."

"What was she doing?" I asked.

"Well, I believe she was looking for you, Madame Rose."

I stared at his grimy face.

"But she thinks I'm with Violette, or on my way there."

He pursed his lips together.

"She's a bright girl, Madame Rose. You know that. She won't be taken in that easily."

He was right, of course. A few weeks ago, Alexandrine had supervised the packing up and removal of my furniture and valises with an eagle eye.

"Are you truly going to your daughter's place, Madame Rose?" she had asked nonchalantly, bent over one of my cases as she struggled to close it with Germaine's help.

And I had replied, even more nonchalantly, gazing at the darker patch on the wall where the oval mirror used to hang:

"Well, of course I am. But first I shall spend some time with the Baronne de Vresse. Germaine is going down to my daughter's with most of my luggage."

Alexandrine had shot a keen eye in my direction. Her grating voice hurt my ears:

"Now, that is unusual, Madame Rose. Because I was with the Baronne recently, delivering her roses, and she never once mentioned you were coming to stay with her."

I was not to be deterred. No matter how

much I was fond of the girl (and believe me, Armand, I am far more attached to that odd creature and her button mouth than to my own daughter), I simply could not let her tamper with my plans. So I tried another tactic. I took her long slim hand in mine and patted her wrist.

"Now, now, Alexandrine, what do you think an old woman like me would do in an empty house on a closed-down street? I have no choice but to go to the Baronne's and then to my daughter's. And that is what I shall do. Trust me."

She glared down at me.

"I will try to trust you, Madame Rose. I will try."

To Gilbert, I said worriedly:

"She somehow learned from my daughter that I have not yet arrived . . . And the Baronne has informed her, I presume, that I never did come and stay. Oh, dear . . ."

"We could always move somewhere else," suggested Gilbert. "There are a couple of places I know. Warmer and more comfortable."

"No," I said quickly. "I will never leave this house. Never."

He sighed ruefully.

"Yes, I know that, Madame Rose. But you should step outside this evening, to see what is going on. I will darken my lantern. The condemned areas are not watched as closely since the cold set in. We won't be bothered. It's icy, but if you hang on to my arm you'll be safe."

"What is it you want me to see, Gilbert?"

He gave me that crooked, rather charming grin.

"You may want to say good-bye to the rue Childebert and the rue Erfurth. Do you not?"

I swallowed with difficulty.

"Yes, you are right, I do."

We set out on a sort of expedition, he and I. He bundled me up as if we were heading for the North Pole. I wore an unknown bedraggled greatcoat which reeked so much of anise and wormwood that I suspected it had been drenched with absinthe, and a top-heavy fur cap, caked with grime, but that kept me warm. No doubt it had belonged, in other times, to a friend of the Baronne de Vresse or such like. When we stepped outside, the cold reached out to envelop me in an icy embrace. It made me gasp with surprise. I could not see a thing, the street was too obscure. It reminded me of those ink-black nights before the public lighting was installed, when walking home even in a safe part of the city became frightening. Gilbert raised his lantern and slid it open so that the dimmed blaze fell softly around us. Our breaths rose in great puffs of white above our heads. I was bracing myself, expecting the crater I had seen when Émile's house had been swallowed by the hungry boulevard. I squinted through the gloom to get a better look.

The row of houses in front of ours had gone. They had been razed to the ground and, believe me, it was stupefying to behold. In their place rose mountains of rubble that had not been disposed of yet. Madame Godfin's boutique was a stack of timber. Madame Barou's building had one flimsy partition still standing. The printing house had vanished into thin air. Monsieur Monthier's chocolate shop was a mass of charred wood. Chez Paulette had disintegrated into a mound of stones. On our side of the street houses still stood bravely, but they bore a new frailty that made me wince. Most of the windows had been broken, at least the ones which had not been shuttered. The façades were all plastered with expropriation orders and decrees. Litter and papers lined the once-clean cobblestones. It was heartbreaking, dearest.

We walked slowly down the deserted, strangely silent street. The freezing air seemed to thicken around us. My shoes slid on the frosty pavement but Gilbert gripped me to him very firmly despite his limp. It struck me again how tall he was. When we got to the bottom of the street, I could not help but let out a gasp of shock. The rue Erfurth had entirely disappeared, all the way down to the rue des Ciseaux. There was nothing left of it, just clutter and debris. All the familiar boutiques and shops had gone, the bench I used to sit on with Maman Odette, even the water fountain had been taken away. Suddenly I felt dizzy, as if I no longer understood where I was. I had lost my bearings. Gilbert asked me gently if I was all right. I nodded helplessly. You know, sometimes the years catch up with me, and I feel the old lady that I am. Believe me, tonight my nearly sixty years weigh heavily upon me.

I could now see where the boulevard Saint-Germain would continue its monstrous sweep, right there, just by the side of the church. Our dark row of houses, where no windows were lit, fragile roofs etched out against the pale wintry sky where no stars glittered, were the last ones standing. It was as if a giant had lumbered out here, and with a huge, clumsy hand, like an angry child, he had knocked away the little streets I had known all my life.

And yet, just beyond the destructions, people were living in houses that still stood, that were safe. People were eating, drinking and sleeping, leading their everyday, ordinary existences, celebrating birthdays, weddings and christenings. The work that went on here was probably a nuisance to them — the mud, the dust, the noise — but at least, their houses were not threatened. They would never know what it meant to lose a beloved house. I felt swamped with sadness and my eyes watered. And then my hatred for the Prefect rose again within me, so powerful, so strong, that if it had not been for Gilbert's sturdy hand, I would have tumbled headfirst onto the thin layer of snow.

When we returned to the house, I was weary. Gilbert must have seen it, for he stayed with me well into the night. A gentleman from the rue des Canettes that he knew and who gave him money and food from time to time had offered soup tonight. We sipped it with relish, the burning liquid filling us up. I could not help thinking of Alexandrine, her coming all the way to this closed-off, condemned part of the area to look for me. My heart went out to her. It had been risky slipping into the abandoned streets, ducking under the wooden barriers that all bore menacing signs of "No trespassing" and "Danger." What was she expecting? I wondered. To find me enjoying a cup of tea in my deserted living room? Had she guessed I was using her cellar as my secret hiding place? She must have suspected something, otherwise she would not have been back here. Gilbert was right. She was a bright girl. How I missed her.

A couple of weeks ago, just as the entire street was packing up in view of the upcoming demolitions, we had spent the morning together, she and I, walking in the Luxembourg Gardens. She had found a position in a large flower shop near the Palais Royal.

"I'm none too pleased about it, the owner of the shop is apparently as bossy as I am," she explained as we walked around the flower beds, "and sparks will fly, but it will do perfectly for the moment, and it is reasonably paid."

"Have you found new lodgings?" I asked.

"Indeed, two large, sunny rooms, near the Louvre. Of course, I will miss the rue Childebert, Madame Rose, but am I not a modern-minded young lady, who approves of what the Prefect is doing to our city?"

I stopped in my steps, gazing across at her, as she is as tall as I am.

"Come, now, my dear girl, I cannot believe for one minute you approve of the new Bois de Boulogne near La Muette?"

She nodded vehemently, her black bonnet

almost sliding off.

"Yes, I do, and I find the new lake positively gorgeous."

I groaned. I thought the Bois de Boulogne was vulgar and you would have too, had you seen it. How could that modern, hilly place full of brash new trees ever compare to the ancient Medicis splendor of our own Luxembourg?

Eight years ago, Alexandrine had not even minded the annexation of the suburbs, the fact that our eleventh arrondissement was now the sixth. You would not have liked that either. Paris became gigantic, tentacular! It now had twenty arrondissements and gained over four hundred thousand Parisians overnight. Our city wolfed up Passy, Auteuil, Batignolles-Monceau, Vaugirard, Grenelle, Montmartre, but also places I had never been to and that were now part of Paris, such as Belleville, La Villette, Bercy and Charonne. I found it puzzling and frightening.

Despite our differences, it was always interesting to converse with Alexandrine. Of course, she was headstrong, and she did sometimes take off in a huff, always coming back, however, to beg my pardon. I grew inordinately fond of her. Yes, she was like another daughter, a warm-hearted, intelligent, cultivated one. Do you find me unfair? I suspect you may. But you must understand how far away Violette has grown for me, both physically and mentally. Another reason that endeared Alexandrine to me all the more was that she was born the same year as Baptiste. 1839. I had told her about our son, but only once. It was too painful to pronounce those words.

I sometimes wonder why she has no husband. Is it her fiery personality? The fact that she says exactly what she thinks and that being submissive is an impossible feat for her to manage? Perhaps. She confessed to me she did not miss having a family, a child. She even admitted that looking after a husband is the last thing she wants. I find such opinions unbelievably different, almost shocking. But then, Alexandrine is not like any other person I know. She has not revealed much about her childhood in Montrouge. Her father took to the bottle and was not kind. Her mother died when she was still young. So you see, I am, in a way, her maman.

I mentioned recently that after your departure two people saved my life. You were no doubt surprised by this declaration. You probably wondered what I meant. I shall now explain. (Just a small interruption: Gilbert is snoring in the most extraordinary fashion. I am tucked away in the cellar, as snug as can be, a piping-hot brick in my lap, and he is upstairs by the enamel cooker. Yet I can still hear him, can you imagine? I have not heard a man snore for a long time. Since your death. It is an odd yet comforting sound.)

Remember the story of the pink card, sent up one morning? The pink card that smelled of roses? I went down to Alexandrine for the first time, and she was waiting for me in the small sitting room behind the boutique, not far from where I am writing to you now.

She had prepared the most delicious meal. A delicate lemon sponge cake, and some wafers, strawberries and cream. And a most excellent tea, a smoked kind I had never tasted before. She told me it came from China. It was called Lapsang souchong and she had purchased it from a new fashionable tea shop in the Marais, Mariage Frères.

I was nervous at first, we had had a rather bad start, remember, but she was most charming with me.

"Do you like flowers, Madame Rose?" she asked.

I had to admit to her that I knew nothing about them, but that I found them lovely.

"Well, that's a start!" she said with a laugh. "And with a name like yours, how could you not like flowers?"

After our meal, she asked if I wanted to stay in the shop for a while, to see how she worked. I was surprised at her offer, but rather flattered to think that this young lady should find my company amusing. So she got me a chair and I sat by the counter and did my embroidery, but to tell you the truth, Armand, I did not get much of that embroidery done, because what I saw and heard on that first day was fascinating.

First of all, as I told you, the shop was delightful, so cheerful, a treat for the eyes. I felt most at ease surrounded by the pink walls, the array of flowers, the intoxicating perfume. Alexandrine had an apprentice with her, a youngster called Blaise, who did not say much, but who was a hard worker.

To my surprise, there was much to be done in a flower shop. You see, flowers are given for so many occasions, for so many reasons. All afternoon I observed Alexandrine adroitly handling her irises, her tulips, her lilies. Her hands were sure and quick. She wore a long black pinafore that gave her a strict elegance. Blaise hovered behind her, his eyes watching every move. They barely talked. Occasionally he went off with a bouquet, to deliver it nearby.

There was never a dull moment. In swept the most dashing gentleman, with curled hair and a flowing black cape, who wanted a gardenia for his buttonhole to wear at the opera that night. Then a lady wished to order flowers for a christening, and another (who brought tears to my eyes, all in black, pale and tired) for a funeral. The young priest who worked with Père Levasque came in to choose lilies for the reopening of the church after two years of restorations. Madame Paccard dropped by for her regular weekly order, as she had fresh flowers put in for every new client at the Hôtel Belfort. Monsieur Helder wanted special floral arrangements for a surprise birthday party in his restaurant on the rue Erfurth.

Each time, and with each client, Alexandrine listened carefully, gave suggestions, listened again, proffered a flower, or another, imagined a bouquet, described it, listened once more. She took her time, and even if a line formed in her shop, she quickly would get another chair, offer a bonbon or a cup of tea and the next customer would wait patiently by my side. No wonder this new shop was doing so well, I thought, compared with the one run by old-fashioned, dreary Madame Collévillé.

There were so many questions I burned to ask Alexandrine as she rushed around the shop. Where did she get her flowers? How did she choose them? Why had she become a florist? But she moved so fast that I could never get a word in. I could only watch her, my hands idle in my lap, as she got on with her day's work.

The next morning I was back. I knocked timidly at the window and she nodded, beckoning me to enter. "You see, Madame Rose, your chair is waiting for you!" she said with a flourish, and it seemed to me that her voice was less grating, that it even had a certain charm to it. All night long I had thought of the flower shop, Armand. And once I was awake, I longed to get back to it, and to her. I began to understand the rhythm of her day. In the mornings, when the fresh flowers had been fetched by her and Blaise at the market, she would point out divine dark red roses to me.

"Look, Madame Rose, these are so lovely that they will go in a flash. They are called Rosa Amadis and no one can resist them."

And she was right. No one could resist those sumptuous roses, their heady perfume, their rich color, their downy texture. By noon there was not one single Rosa Amadis left in the shop. They had all gone.

"People adore roses," Alexandrine explained, as she prepared ready-made bouquets for customers to purchase on their way home or to a dinner. "Roses are the queen of flowers. You cannot go wrong when you offer a rose."

As we spoke, she had already made three or four bouquets. Each was completely different, created with various sorts of flowers, foliage and strands of satin ribbons. It seemed effortless. But I knew it was not. She had a way with flowers, that young woman.

One morning Alexandrine appeared to be in a state of excitement. She snapped at poor Blaise, who got on with his tasks like a brave little soldier facing the enemy. I wondered what could have caused such turmoil. She kept staring at the clock on the wall, opening the door that gave on the street, the bell giving a little chime each time, standing on the pavement, hands on hips, glancing up and down the rue Childebert. I was mystified. Who could she be waiting for? A fiancé? A special delivery?

And then all of a sudden, when I felt I could no longer stand the wait, a figure appeared on the threshold of the shop. The loveliest woman I had ever seen.

She floated into the boutique as if she had been walking on a cloud. Oh, my dear, how can I ever begin to describe her? Even Blaise knelt in reverence. She was exquisite, tiny, a porcelain doll. Of course, she wore the latest fashions. A mauve crinoline (the Empress wore nothing but mauve that year) with a white lace collar and cuffs, and her bonnet was the prettiest contraption you could imagine. She came with a maid, who waited outside, as it was a sunny spring afternoon.

I could not take my eyes off this enchanting stranger. Her face was a perfect oval, she had beautiful black eyes, creamy white skin, pearly teeth and glossy black hair raised in a braided bun. I had no idea who she was, but I immediately guessed she was most important to Alexandrine. She held out her hands to her, and Alexandrine declaimed, clasping those tiny white hands to her in adoration:

"Oh, madame, I thought you wouldn't ever come!"

The lovely stranger threw her head back and laughed gaily.

"Now, now, mademoiselle, I had word sent to you that I'd be here at ten, and here I am, only a few minutes late! We have so much to do, have we not? I'm certain you have come up with splendid ideas for me!"

I stared, entranced. So did Blaise, whose mouth was open.

"Oh, I have had the most superb ideas, madame. Just wait till I show you. But first of all, let me introduce you to my landlady, Madame Bazelet."

The lady turned to me with a gracious smile. I got up to greet her.

"Her name is Rose," Alexandrine pursued. "Do you not find that delightful?"

"Oh, indeed! Positively delightful!"

"Madame Rose, this is my best and most wonderful client, the Baronne de Vresse."

The tiny white hand pressed mine, and then, at Alexandrine's signal, Blaise dashed to get papers and sketches from the back room, and they were laid on the large table with care. I longed to know what all this regarded.

I began to understand as the Baronne carefully described a dress. A ball dress. My dear, it was the grandest event. The Baronne was attending a ball given by the Empress herself. The Princess Mathilde was to attend, and the Prefect and his wife, and all sorts of elegant people.

Alexandrine acted as if all this were perfectly normal, but I was beside myself with excitement. The dress was being made by Worth, of course, that famous couturier on the rue de la Paix where all the fashionable ladies went. The Baronne's dress was flaming pink, she told us, with round shoulders, a frilly bertha, and the crinoline had five full flounces and a layer of tassels. Alexandrine showed her the sketches. She had imagined a slim wreath of pink rosebuds, mother-of-pearl and rhinestones for the Baronness's coiffure and corsage.

Such adorable drawings! I was impressed by Alexandrine's creative talent. No wonder ladies flocked to her boutique. You are probably wondering why I, always so critical of the Empress and her frivolities, could harbor such admiration toward the Baronne de Vresse. I will be honest with you, dearest, she was charming. There was nothing shallow or empty about her. She asked my advice, several times, as if it meant something to her, as if I were an important personage. I do not know how old this captivating creature was — in her twenties, I presumed? — but I could tell she had had an impeccable education, she spoke several languages, she had traveled the world. The Empress too? No doubt. Ah, but you would have adored the lovely Baronne. I know it.

At the end of the day, I knew a little bit more about the Baronne de Vresse, born Louise de Villebague, who had married Felix de Vresse at just eighteen. I learned she had two little girls, Bérénice and Apolline. I heard she loved flowers, and that she daily filled her house on the rue Taranne with them. I knew Alexandrine was the only flower lady she wanted to work with, because Mademoiselle Walcker truly "understands flowers," she said gravely, looking at me with those black, shining eyes.

I must stop for now, my sweet. My hand aches from all this writing. Gilbert's snore is a comforting sound. It makes me feel safe. I shall now curl up into all those blankets and sleep as much as I possibly can.

Such strange dreams I have been having. The latest one is decidedly odd. I was lying down in a kind of flattened meadow, staring up at the sky. It was a particularly warm day and my thick wintry dress felt itchy next to my skin. The ground below my body was sumptuously soft, and when I turned my head I realized I was lying atop a thick bed of rose petals. Some of them were crushed and wilted and they set off a delicious perfume. I could hear a young girl singing gently, not too far away. She sounded like Alexandrine, although I could not be sure. I wanted to get up but found I was unable to. My hands and feet were tied together by slender silk ribbons. I could not speak, my mouth was covered with a cotton scarf. I tried to struggle, but my movements were sluggish and ponderous, as if I had been drugged. So I lay there, helpless. I was not afraid. The heat bothered me the most, the sun shining onto my pale skin did too. If I stayed here any longer, I would become freckled. The chanting grew louder, and I heard the thump of footsteps, muffled by the rose petals. A face looked down at mine and I could not make out who it was, as the sun glowed too strongly. Then I recognized a girl I had seen in the bookstore many times, a disturbed child, with the round face of a cretin. She was a gentle, pathetic creature, I cannot recall her name, but I believe she had some sort of secret link to Monsieur Zamaretti, the bookshop owner, a link that he did not wish to divulge. When I came in to choose my books, she was often there, sitting on the floor, playing with a soft balloon. Sometimes I showed her pictures from the Comtesse de Ségur tales. She would laugh, or rather she howled, very loudly, but I became accustomed to it. There she was, in my dream, dangling daisies on my forehead, howling with laughter. I tried to explain to her how to untie me, but she did not understand. I became flustered, the sun was burning, scorching me. I lost my temper, I shouted at her, and she grew frightened. She backed away despite my pleas, and she took off, breaking into a clumsy, animal-like run. She disappeared. I shouted, but the scarf around my mouth prevented me from being heard. And I did not even know her name. I felt helpless. I burst into tears, and when I awoke from this dream, there were tears running down my cheeks.

Rue Childebert, March 18th, 1865

My very dear Madame Rose,

This is the first letter ever I am writing to you, but somehow I can tell it will not be the last. Germaine has come down to inform me that you are not coming to the shop this afternoon because of a bad cold. I am so sorry and I shall miss you so! Do get well soon.

I am putting pen to paper as Blaise gets on with the first orders of the day, and I will send this letter up to you once I have finished it. It is chilly down here this morning and I'm rather relieved to think that you are tucked up in bed, all snug and warm, with Mariette and Germaine to dote upon you. I am so accustomed to your presence here with me that I cannot bear to look at the empty seat in the corner where you sit with your embroidery. All the customers will ask after you, you can be sure of that. But the one who will be the most upset will be our divine Baronne. She will ask Blaise where you are, what is wrong, and she is bound to send a little gift back with him, a book maybe, or maybe those chocolates we are both so fond of.

I do so much enjoy our conversations. I never did talk much to my parents. My father preferred his eau de vie over his daughter, or his wife, and my mother was not the loving kind. I must admit I grew up a lonely child. I feel that somehow you are a sort of mother to me. I hope this does not disturb you. You already have a daughter, and like you, she bears a name that is a flower's name, but I am led to believe that you are not terribly close to her. You have taken up a new and important place in my life, Madame Rose, and as I gaze at your empty chair today, I feel it strongly. However, there is another matter about which I wish to confer with you at present. It is a tricky one, and I am not certain how to go about it. I shall try.

You are aware of where I stand concerning the Prefect's works upon our city. I consider them a necessary progress and I fully comprehend that this is not the case for you. But you see, I must unburden myself with what I know. You are firmly convinced that our neighborhood is protected, that the embellishments will spare your family home because of the proximity of the church. Now, I am not so sure of that. I see what is being done to our city. I do approve of these changes. (We will not quarrel again about the Prefect because you have a cold, so I will drop that matter here and now.) However, I beg you to start thinking about what might happen if you do receive word that your house is to be pulled down. (I know this will make you wince and that you shall hate me. But I care about you too much, Madame Rose, to fret about a passing resent.)

Do you recall when you helped me deliver those white lilies to the place de Furstenberg, when the painter Delacroix died in his studio? (A couple of years ago.) Whilst we were in the studio, arranging the flowers, I overheard a gentleman talking to another. I never told you this because I did not want to bother you. And I never believed that your house would be in danger. But now that I have witnessed how fast the works are going, their tremendous pace, their massive organization, I do sense danger. One gentleman (elegant, well-to-do person, with twirling mustache and well-pressed suit) was talking to another (younger, less important, obviously) about the Prefect and his team. I was not listening with great attention, but I did catch this: "I've seen the layout at the Hôtel de Ville. Those small, dark streets around the church, right around the corner from here, are going to go. Too humid, too narrow. Good thing old Delacroix isn't around anymore to see that."

I thought then, as I led you out of the building onto the rue de l'Abbaye, that this would take a while to be acted out. I also believed that perhaps the rue Childebert was not included, as it was indeed so near the church. But I now realize that this may not be the case. Oh, Madame Rose, I am afraid.

I am sending this letter up now with Blaise, and I beg you to read it to the end. We need to think about what will happen if worse comes to worst. We have time yet, but not that much time.

I am sending up a little bouquet of your favorite roses. The pink ones. Every time I handle them, smell them, sell them, I think of you.

Your affectionate,
Alexandrine

Hardly any aches this morning. I am astonished at how sturdy my body is. At my age!
Do you think it is because I am young at
heart? Because I am not afraid? Because I
know you are waiting for me? Outside, a
pale sun is shining. The cold has deepened.
There is no snow. Only the sunshine and
blue sky I can see from the kitchen window.
Our city, or rather that of the Emperor and
the Prefect, is at its best under the winter
sun. Oh, I'm perfectly happy not to lay eyes
on those boulevards anymore. Did I not
read a while ago what one of the Goncourt
brothers wrote about them? "The new
boulevards, so long, so large, so geometric,
as boring as endless roads." How I had
chuckled!

Alexandrine had dragged me, one summer evening, to walk along the new boulevards behind the Madeleine church. It had
been a hot, stuffy day, and I longed for the

cool serenity of my living room, but she would not hear of it. She made me put on a pretty dress (the ruby and black one), readjust my chignon and slip my feet into those tiny boots you used to love. Frankly, an elegant old lady like me, I needed to go out and see the world, instead of staying at home with my tisane and my mohair blanket! Did I not live in a beautiful city? Did I not want to be out tonight with her on the town, instead of alone, at home? I let myself be gently bullied.

We took a crowded omnibus to get there. I cannot tell you how many human beings lined those long new avenues. Could Paris hold that many citizens? We could hardly pick our way along the brand-new sidewalks dotted with chestnut trees. And the noise, Armand. The constant roll of wheels, the clattering of hooves. Voices and laughter. Newspaper vendors yelling out their trade. Flower girls proffering violets. The blaze of shop lights, of the new streetlamps. It was like being in the middle of the day. Imagine an endless stream of carriages and passersby. Everyone seemed to be parading, showing off finery, jewelry, a sophisticated hat, an ample bosom, the curve of hips. Red lips, curled coiffures, sparkling stones. Boutiques exposed their goods in a dazzling profusion of choice, fabrics and colors. Luminous cafés spilled their customers out onto the pavement in rows and rows of little tables, with waiters speedily rushing in and out, trays held high.

Alexandrine fought boldly to get a table (I would never have dared) and we finally managed to sit down, a group of loud gentlemen right behind us, knocking back their beers. We ordered prune liqueur. On our right, two very rouged ladies preened themselves. I noticed their décolletage and their dyed hair. Alexandrine rolled her eyes at me discreetly. We knew what they were and what they were waiting for. And soon enough, one of the men from a nearby table lolled over, bent to murmur a few words. A few minutes later he staggered off, a creature on each arm, accompanied by the cheers and whistles of his companions. *Revolting,* mouthed Alexandrine. I nodded and took a sip of my liqueur.

The more I sat there, a helpless spectator to the flow of vulgarity, the angrier I became. I glanced up at the huge, pale buildings facing us on the monotonously straight avenue. Not a light burning in luxurious apartments built for citizens who had money. The Prefect and the Emperor had built a stage décor, to their image. It had no heart, it had no soul.

"Isn't it grand?" murmured Alexandrine, her eyes wide. As I looked at her, I could not bring myself to voice my own discontent. She was young and enthusiastic, and she loved this new Paris, like all the people around us, reveling in the summer evening. She was soaking up the tawdriness, the display, the shallowness.

Oh, what had become of my medieval city, its quaint charm, its sinuous dark alleys? It seemed to me that tonight Paris had turned into a florid, overripe harlot flaunting her froufrous.

By my side is a stack of books. They are most precious to me. Yes, books. Now I hear you chuckling. Let me tell you at last how this happened. And you will understand why Monsieur Zamaretti, after Alexandrine, became that second important person to give a new meaning to my life.

One day, as I was leaving the flower shop, my head full of scents, colors and petals, of Baronne de Vresse's ball gowns, Monsieur Zamaretti asked me most politely to visit his boutique whenever I had a free moment. (He had of course noticed how Alexandrine's recent decorations had helped her commerce to flourish, and he had decided to redesign his own shop. I had never been in there, although I know you had, as you were fond of reading. Monsieur Zamaretti had also noticed that I spent many hours with Alexandrine, since the past couple of years. Was he not a mite envious of our friendship? He had once popped in on a rainy June day, when Alexandrine and her clients were gossiping about the sensational execution at the Roquette prison of young Docteur Couty-Pommerais, who was accused of poisoning his mistress. Masses of people had gone to watch the man being guillotined. Monsieur Zamaretti gave us all sorts of gory details, as one of his friends had actually witnessed the beheading from very close up. The more we shrieked with horror, the more he seemed to be enjoying himself.)

I accepted his invitation, and went to the bookstore one afternoon. The first thing I noticed as I walked in was the intoxicating smell of leather and paper. It was pleasing. He had done a very decent job. The walls were pale blue, most soothing, and one could sit down in comfortable armchairs under good lamps and read to one's heart's content. Monsieur Zamaretti had a high wooden desk covered with pencils, notebooks, magnifying glasses, letters and clippings. His shop was longer and darker than Alexandrine's, the atmosphere was studious and intellectual. There were rows of books of all sizes and colors, and there was a long ladder in order to reach them.

Alexandrine's boutique was full of chatter

and noise, the rustle of the paper she used to wrap the flowers up, the clang of the bell at the door, Blaise's frequent cough. Here, silence reigned. I noticed a gentleman in a corner, reading quietly. It was almost like entering a church. I congratulated Monsieur Zamarreti on his taste and was about to take my leave. And then he asked the same question that Alexandrine had, all those months ago. Except, of course, his query regarded his trade, not hers.

"Do you like to read, Madame Rose?"

I was taken aback. I did not know what to say. Of course, it is embarrassing, is it not, to have to admit one does not read. One comes across as an idiot. So I mumbled a few words and looked down at my shoes.

"Perhaps you would like to sit here and read for a while?" he suggested, with that smooth smile of his. (He is not good-looking, as you recall, but one must point out his hazel eyes and white teeth, and the fact that he dresses with great care. You know how fond I am of detailing clothes, and I can tell you that on that day he was wearing dark blue checked trousers, a purple and pink check waistcoat and a frock coat trimmed with astrakhan.) He ushered me to one of the armchairs and made sure the lamp was turned on. I sat down meekly.

"As I do not know your tastes, may I make a couple of suggestions for today?"

I nodded. He beamed, and clambered nimbly up the ladder. I admired his emerald-green socks. He came down again, carefully balancing a couple of books on his hip.

"We have a few authors here that I'm certain you might like. Paul de Kock, Balzac, Dumas, Erckmann-Chatrian . . ."

He placed the leather-bound volumes with their titles in gold lettering on the little table on front of me. *The Barber of Paris. L'Ami Fritz. The Black Tulip. The Colonel Chabert.* I looked at them dubiously, biting my lip.

"Oh!" he suddenly exclaimed. "I have an idea."

Up he rushed again. This time he reached out for one book only. He handed it to me as soon as his feet touched the ground.

"I know you will love this one, Madame Rose."

I took it gingerly. It was rather thick, I noticed with a sinking heart.

"What is it about?" I asked politely.

"It is about a young woman. She is beautiful and bored. She is married to a doctor and she is stifled by the banality of her provincial existence."

I noticed that the silent reader from across

the room had lifted his head, nodded and was listening intently.

"And what happens to this beautiful, bored lady?" I asked, curious in spite of myself.

Monsieur Zamaretti glanced down at me as if he were reeling in a promising catch on a good fishing day.

"You see, this young woman is an avid reader of sentimental novels. She longs for romance and finds her marriage dreary. So she indulges in affairs and tragedy inevitably rears its head —"

"Is this novel suitable for a respectable old lady like myself?" I interrupted.

He gasped with mock horror. (You remember how he has a tendency to exaggerate.)

"Madame Rose! How would your most humble and dignified servant ever dare propose a book that is not fitting to your rank and intelligence? I only dared suggest this one because I happen to know that ladies who are not ardent readers succumb to this book with passion."

"Most probably egged on by the scandal concerning the trial," remarked the solitary reader from the other side of the room. Monsieur Zamaretti jumped as if he had forgotten his very presence. "Everybody wanted to read that book all the more."

"You are indeed right, monsieur. The scandal did help the book sell furiously, it must be said."

"What scandal? What trial?" I asked, feeling foolish once again.

"Well, this must have been three or four years ago, Madame Rose, around the time your husband passed away. The author was charged with outrage to public morals and religion. Full publication of the novel was blocked and this prompted a lawsuit that was very much commented upon by the press. And then everyone wanted to read the novel that had stirred up such a scandal. I myself sold dozens of copies a day."

I looked down at the book, opened the flyleaf.

"And what do you think of it, Monsieur Zamaretti?" I asked.

"I believe that Gustave Flaubert is one of our most greatest authors," he said. "And that *Madame Bovary* is a masterpiece."

"Come, now," scoffed the reader from his corner. "That's going a little too far."

Monsieur Zamaretti ignored him.

"Just read the first few pages, Madame Rose. If you don't like it, you don't have to pursue."

I nodded again, took a deep breath, and

turned to the first page. I was doing this for him, of course. He had been so kind since your death, always sending warm smiles my way, waving to me when I passed his shop. I nestled comfortably in the deep armchair and said to myself that I'd read for twenty minutes. Then I'd thank him and go upstairs.

The next thing I remembered was that Germaine was standing in front of me, wringing her hands. I could not quite recall where I was, nor what I was doing. I seemed to be coming back from another world. Germaine stared down at me, at a loss for words. I suddenly realized I was in the bookshop down below. It was pitch-dark outside and my stomach was rumbling.

"What time is it?" I asked feebly.

"Well, madame, it is getting on for seven o'clock. Mariette and I have been most worried. Dinner is ready and the chicken is fairly overdone. We did not find you in the flower shop and Mademoiselle Walcker said you had been gone for ages."

She looked intently at the book I held in my hands. Then I understood that I had been reading for over three hours. Monsieur Zamaretti helped me up. His was a smile of triumph.

"Would you like to come back tomorrow

and continue your read?" he asked mellifluously.

"Yes," I replied in a daze. I let myself be led upstairs by a stern Germaine, who kept clicking her tongue and shaking her head.

"Is Madame all right?" whispered Mariette, hovering by the door, surrounded by the tempting scent of roast chicken.

"Madame is fine," snapped Germaine. "Madame was reading. She forgot everything else."

I think you would have laughed, my love.

Little by little, I ended up spending my mornings in the bookshop and my afternoons with Alexandrine. Studious mornings when I read for a couple of hours, then up to a quick luncheon prepared by Mariette and served by Germaine, then down again to the flower shop. You see now how reading and flowers became my personal patterns, became the secret way I was able to hold on to life after you left.

I simply could not wait to get back to Charles, Emma, Léon and Rodolphe. The book was waiting for me on the little table in front of the armchair and I rushed to it with haste. It is not easy to explain how I felt while I read, but I will try. No doubt you, as a reader, will understand. It appeared I found myself in a place where no one could bother me, where no one could reach me. I grew impervious to all the noises around me, Monsieur Zamaretti's voice, that of other clients, passersby on the street. Even when the retarded little girl came to play, and howled with laughter as she rolled her ball along the floor, I only saw the words on the page. The sentences turned into images that I was magically drawn into. The images flowed through my head. Emma and her black hair and black eyes, so black they were at times almost blue. The minute details of her life made me feel like I was standing by her side, living those moments with her. Her first ball at La Vaubyessard, her giddying waltz with the Viscount. The stagnant rhythm of her country life, her rising discontent. Her inner dreams, rendered so vividly. Rodolphe, the ride in the woods, her surrender, the secret rendezvous in the garden. Then the affair with Léon in the faded splendor of a hotel room. And the horrific end which left me gasping, the blood, the pain, Charles's grief.

How could I have waited so long to discover the joys of reading? Now I remember how concentrated you were during those winter evenings when you would read by the fireplace. I sewed, or darned, or wrote letters. Sometimes I played a game of dominoes. And still you would remain in your seat, your book in your hands, your eyes roving from page to page. I remember thinking that reading was your favorite pastime and that I did not share it. It did not worry me. I knew my own favorite pastime was clothes and fashion, and that you did not share that with me either. Whilst I marveled at the cut of a dress or the tint of a fabric, you reveled in Plato, Honoré de Balzac, Alexandre Dumas and Eugène Sue. Oh, my love, how you felt close to me as I devoured *Madame Bovary*. I could not think what the fuss had been about, concerning the trial. Had Flaubert not managed to place himself precisely within Emma Bovary's mind, making his reader undergo every sensation she experienced, her boredom, her pain, her sorrow, her rapture?

One morning, very early, Alexandrine took me to the flower market at Saint-Sulpice. I had asked Germaine to rouse me at three in the morning. She had done so, her face puffy with sleep, whilst I felt excitement tingling through me and no tiredness whatsoever. I was at last going to find out how Alexandrine chose her flowers. She did this on Tuesdays and Fridays, with Blaise. There we were, the three of us, in the dark and silent rue Childebert. No one was about, only a couple of ragpickers with their hooks and lanterns. They scuffled away when they saw us. I do not believe I had ever laid eyes on my city at such an early hour. Had you?

We walked down the rue des Ciseaux, and there, on the rue des Canettes, the first wagons and carts heading to the square in front of the church could be seen. Alexandrine had explained to me recently that the Prefect was having a new market built near Saint-Eustache Church, a huge construction with glass and metal pavilions, no doubt a monstrosity, and this would be ready this year or the next, but you can imagine I had not had the heart to go there. Nor did I want to behold the construction works for his grandiose new opera. It was thus to this enormous new market that Alexandrine would have to go for her stock of flowers. But the morning I was telling you about, my dear, we were headed to Saint-Sulpice, where the flower market was held twice a week, as you recall. It was a chilly spring morning, and I pulled my coat around me, wishing I had taken one of my woolen scarves, the pink one. Blaise tugged a wooden chariot behind him, it was almost as large as he was.

As we drew nearer, I could make out the hum of voices and the clatter of wheels on cobblestones. The gas lamps above the tents created bright pockets of light over each stall. The familiar, soft scent of flowers greeted me like a friend's embrace. We followed Alexandrine through a colorful maze of flowers. She named them all for me as we passed. Carnations, snowdrops, tulips, violets, camellias, forget-me-nots, lilac, narcissus, anemones, ranunculus . . . I felt like she was introducing me to her best friends. "It's too early yet in the season for peonies," she chirped. "But once they start coming in, you'll see they are nearly as popular as roses."

Alexandrine wove through the displays with a brisk, professional manner. She knew exactly what she wanted. The vendors greeted her by her first name, and some of the men were overtly flirtatious, but she was having none of that. She barely smiled. She turned up her nose at clusters of small round white roses that I thought lovely. When she noticed I appeared puzzled, she pointed out they lacked freshness.

"Aimée Vibert white roses need to be just perfect," she whispered. "They need to look like fine white silk, tinged at the edges with the faintest trace of pink. We use them for wedding bouquets, you see. These here will not last."

How could she tell? I wondered. I suppose it was to do with the way the petals curled and the tint of the stems? I felt giddy but elated, watching her finger leaves and petals with that deft sure touch, sometimes bringing her nose down for a whiff or letting petals caress her cheek. She entered tough negotiations with the vendors. I was taken aback by her fortitude. Not once did she relent, not once did she back down. She was twenty-five years old and yet she had the upper hand over middle-aged hard-boiled traders.

I wondered where the great mass of flowers came from.

"From the Midi," answered Blaise, "from the south and the sun."

I could not help thinking of the stream of flowers pouring into the city, day after day. And where did they all go once they were sold?

"Balls, churches, weddings and graveyards," answered Alexandrine, as Blaise steadfastly stacked the flowers she had purchased into the chariot. "Paris is always hungry for flowers, Madame Rose. The city needs her ration, every day. Flowers for love, flowers for sorrow, flowers for joy, flowers to remember. Flowers for friends."

I asked why she had decided to take on this profession. She smiled, patting the heavy coil of hair piled upon her head.

"There was a large garden near where we lived, in Montrouge. It was beautiful, with a fountain and a statue. I used to play there every morning, and the gardeners working there taught me all about flowers. It was fascinating. I'd watch them and learn. I quickly understood that flowers would end up being part of my life." Then she added, in a low voice, so only I could hear, "Flowers have a language of their own, Madame Rose. I find it so much more powerful than words." And she promptly tucked a pink rosebud into the buttonhole of my coat.

I imagined her as a child, a tall, thin creature, unruly curls tamed by two braids, roaming the garden in Montrouge, a green place that smelled of mignonettes and roses, bending over buds, long, sensitive hands examining petals, thorns, bulbs, blossoms. She had told me she was a lonely child, no siblings. I could see how flowers became her closest friends.

The sun had by now made a timid appearance over the two towers of Saint-Sulpice. The last gas lamps had been turned down. I felt as if I had been awake for ages. It was time to go back to the rue Childebert. Blaise heaved the cart behind him, and once we got to the shop, the flowers were adroitly arranged into vases of water.

Very soon the bell at the door would start to tinkle, and Alexandrine's flowers would make their magical, perfumed way around the city. And yet, my flower girl remained a mystery and she still is today. For all these years, and in spite of our long talks and our strolls around the Luxembourg Gardens, I know very little about her. Does she have a young man in her life? Is she a married man's mistress? I simply have no idea. Alexandrine is like that fascinating cactus Maman Odette used to own, deceptively smooth and terrifyingly prickly.

I learned to live without you, little by little. I had to. Is it not what widows do? It was another existence. I tried to be brave. I believe I was. Père Levasque, busy with the restoration of his church by one of the Prefect's architects, Monsieur Baltard (the very same man who is at present building the new market I was telling you about), no longer had time to walk around the Luxembourg Gardens with me. I had to fend for myself. I did it, with the help of my new allies. Alexandrine kept me busy. She sent me out on delivery errands with Blaise. We made a fine pair, he and I. We were greeted from the rue de l'Abbaye down to the rue du Four, him with his chariot, and me holding the most precious flowers in my arms.

Our favorite delivery was the Baronne de Vresse's roses. Alexandrine would spend most of the morning choosing them. This took her a while. They had to be the finest, the loveliest, the most fragrant. The pink Adèle Heu roses. The white Aimée Vibert, the ivory Adelaïde d'Orléans or the dark red Amadis. Then they were carefully wrapped up in soft paper and boxes, their stems humid, and we had but little time to rush them over.

The Baronne de Vresse lived in a beautiful, ancient building on the corner of the rue Taranne and the rue du Dragon. The front door was opened by Célestin, the valet. He had a serious face, a disturbing hairy pimple on the side of his nose, and he was utterly devoted to the Baronne. One had to go up a wide flight of stone stairs which always took us a moment, Blaise struggling with the cart and me taking care not to slip on the old flagstones. She never kept us waiting. She patted Blaise's head and slipped him some coins, and she sent him back to the shop and kept me. I watched her take care of the flowers. No one else was allowed to handle her roses. We sat in a large, light room that was her own, her "lair," she called it. It was delightfully simple. No crimson velvet here, no gold gilt, no mirrors, no glittering chandeliers. The walls were pale magenta and there were children's drawings pinned on them. The carpets were soft and white, the canopies covered with toile de Jouy. It was like being in a country house. The Baronne liked her roses to be arranged in tall, slim vases, and there had to be at least three bouquets of them. Sometimes her husband rushed in and out, a lofty, sprightly man who barely acknowledged me, but there was nothing displeasing about him.

I could sit there for hours, basking in the gentle, feminine atmosphere. What did we talk about? you may wonder. Her children, sweet little girls I sometimes glimpsed with their governess. Her social life, which fascinated me, the Mabille ball, the opera, the theaters. And we much discussed books, because, like you, she was a reader. She had read *Madame Bovary* in one single go, to her husband's despair (and annoyance), as she could not have been dragged away from the novel. I had admitted to her that I was a recent reader, that my new hobby was born thanks to Monsieur Zamaretti, whose shop was next to Alexandrine's. We had talks about books, she and I. She suggested Alphonse Daudet and Victor Hugo and I listened to her describe their work with rapture.

How different our existences were, I mused. Did she not have it all, the beauty, the brains, the breeding, the brilliant marriage? Yet I felt a tangible sadness lurking within Louise de Vresse. She was much younger than me, younger than Violette, than Alexandrine, but she possessed a maturity I had rarely seen in a person her age. I wondered, as I admired her lissome figure, what her secrets were. What was there beneath the veneer? I found myself wanting to confide in her and wishing to hear her own divulgences. Of course, I knew how improbable this was.

There was one captivating exchange, I recall. I was sitting with the Baronne one morning after the flower delivery and enjoying a cup of hot chocolate served by Célestin. (Such magnificent Limoges porcelain, stamped with the de Vresse coat of arms.) She was reading the paper next to me and making witty comments about the news. I did like that about her, her keen interest in what went on in the world around us, her natural curiosity. She certainly was no vain, empty-headed coquette. That day she was wearing an enchanting pearl-white crinoline dress with funnel-shaped lace-trimmed sleeves and a high-necked bodice that showed off her slender bust to perfection. "Oh, thank the Lord!" she exclaimed suddenly, bent over the printed page, and I asked her what the matter was. She explained that the Empress in person had intervened to considerably reduce the poet Charles Baudelaire's penalty. Had I read *Les Fleurs du Mal?* she asked. I told her that Monsieur Zamaretti had recently spoken to me about Monsieur Baudelaire. He informed me there had also been a trial and a scandal concerning his poems, like what had happened for *Madame Bovary.* However, I had not read them yet. She got up and went to fetch a slender book in the adjoining room. She handed it to me. *Les Fleurs du Mal.* A beautiful edition in fine green leather with a wreath of exotic, twisted flowers on the cover.

"I think you will enjoy these poems very much, Madame Rose," she said. "Please borrow this copy and read it. I long to know what you think." So I went home and had my luncheon, and then sat down to read the poems. I opened the book warily. The only poems I had ever read were the very private ones you sent me, beloved. I was desperately afraid of being bored as I leafed through the pages. What could I say to the Baronne without hurting her feelings?

Now, I am aware that as a reader one needs to trust the writer, trust the poet. They know how to reach out and pluck us out of our ordinary life and send us careening into another world we have not even fathomed. That is what talented authors do. That is what Monsieur Baudelaire did to me.

Villa Marbella, Biarritz, June 27th, 1865

My dear Madame Rose,

Many thanks for your letter. It took a while to reach me, as I am now in Basque country, staying with Lady Bruce, a dear friend, an Englishwoman of marvelous taste and such good company. I met her a couple of years ago in Paris, at a ladies' luncheon party at the Hôtel de Charost, which as you may know is the British Embassy on the rue Saint-Honoré. The Ambassadress, Lady Cowley, had placed Lady Bruce next to me at table, and we got on splendidly, despite the age difference. I suppose you could say she is old enough to be my grandmother, however, there is nothing old about Lady Bruce, she is amazingly energetic. Nevertheless, your letter is at last here, and I am happy to read you and hear your news. I am also delighted to discover that you have taken such a fancy to Charles Baudelaire! (My husband cannot fathom why I am so besotted with his verse, and I am immensely relieved to find an ally in you.)

Ah, what a joy it was to leave the rue Taranne, dusty, noisy Paris! But I do miss my favorite florist terribly (and her precious companion). Nowhere in this town, despite the scintillating presence of Queen Isabella of Spain, and even the Empress herself, can I find anyone capable of delivering such lovely flowers and creating such enchanting headdresses. What am I to do? For what you must know, dear Madame Rose, is that Biarritz is perhaps even more elegant and brilliant at the moment than the capital itself.

Our stay here is a whirlwind of balls, fireworks, excursions and picnics. Frankly, I would not mind curling up with a simple frock and a book, but Lady Bruce and my husband would not hear of it. (Lady Bruce is quite terrifying when she does not get her own way, you see. She is a mere slip of a woman, half your size, and yet she has utter command over us all. Those pale gray eyes, perhaps, the slim mouth set in such a fierce yet charming manner? Even her step in her tiny pantoufles is the very definition of authority.)

I must tell you about her home, the Villa Marbella. I am sure you would adore it. It is utterly splendid, imagine a marble, ceramic and mosaic Moorish fantasy straight out of *The Arabian Nights.* Imagine slender arcades, tinkling fountains, light-reflecting pools, a shaded patio and a glass dome which sparkles in the sun. And, of course, the view of the beach, and the sea. When ones looks south, there looms Spain! So near, and the peaks of the Pyrénées, always shrouded by fluffy clouds. When one turns north, there is Biarritz and its cliffs and frothy waves.

I love the proximity of the sea, except that it turns my hair atrociously frizzy. I need to have it straightened every evening. Rather tedious, I must say. Especially just before our carriage takes us to the Villa Eugénie. That is where the Empress awaits us, you see, in the magnificent E-shaped mansion you have no doubt read about, that the Emperor built just for her. (I know you follow the fashions closely, and I do believe you would be thrilled by the fabulous dresses worn on those dazzling soirées. Except that those crinolines seem to be getting bigger and bigger and it is becoming a worrying complication to attend parties with such crowds.)

You ask how my little girls are, how sweet of you. Well, Apolline and Bérénice do love it here. I won't have them go too near the sea, as the waves are tremendous. (We heard a young man drowned the other day, at Guéthary. He got caught by the current. A tragedy.)

I took the girls and their governess to an interesting social event earlier this week. The weather was stormy and rainy, but no one minded. A large crowd had gathered by the beach and the port, waiting for the Emperor to turn up. It was rather a squash, but we managed. Just beyond the port and those treacherous waters that trap so many ships lies a huge brown rock that juts out into the choppy sea. On top of that rock, and at the Emperor's demand, a large white statue of the Madonna has been placed as a protector to all those at sea trying to find their way inland. The Emperor and his wife were the first to walk along the slender iron and wooden bridge which led to the rock, amidst much clapping. We soon followed in their wake, and the little ones were impressed by the swell of the waves slapping against the rocky platform. I glanced up at the white face of the Madonna, as she stood there in the breeze, looking out west, toward the Americas. I wondered how long she will stay up there, battling against violent storms, winds and rain.

Do give all my very best to Alexandrine and to Blaise. I shall be back at the end of the season, and I very much hope I shall receive another letter from you before then?

Louise Eglantine de Vresse

I felt the icy hand again and the intruder's breath in my face. The struggle to push him away, the furious, frantic kick and shove of my legs and arms, my muffled scream as he squashed his filthy palm onto my mouth. The dreadful moment when I understand that my struggle is in vain and that he will have his way. The only manner to keep the nightmare at bay is to write to you. I am tired, so tired, my love. I want the end to come. I know it is near. Yet there is more to tell you. I need to straighten out my thoughts. I am afraid of confusing you all the more. My strength is not going to hold out much longer. I am too old to be living in such conditions. Yet you know that nothing will ever make me leave this house.

I feel slightly better now. A couple hours of sleep, even if they were short, have rejuvenated me. It is time now to tell you about my battle against the Prefect, about what I endeavored. I want to relate everything I tried to do to save our house. After the letter came last year, I noticed little by little how our neighbors reacted differently. Only Madame Paccard, Docteur Nonant and myself had decided to put up a fight.

What you must know is that last year the winds began to turn, despite the success of the Exposition Universelle. The Prefect was no longer haloed by an aura of glory. After fifteen grueling years of destructions, a slow murmur of discontent had begun, at first unnoticed, and then louder and louder still. I read harsh articles concerning him in the press by Monsieur Picard and Monsieur Ferry, both very virulent. Everyone seemed to question the financing of the embellishments, the extent of the work. Had the Prefect been right to raze the Ile de la Cité? To undergo such massive destructions in the Latin Quarter? Had he not been heavy-handed? And how had he financed all this, exactly? And then, you see, in the midst of this turmoil, the Prefect made two faux pas. I believe they shall cost him his honor. Time will tell.

The first mistake concerned our beloved Luxembourg. (Oh, dearest, how you would have lost your temper over this. I can only too well imagine you spluttering over your morning coffee as you discovered the matter-of-fact decree in the paper.) It was a chilly November day and Germaine was busy with the fire as I read the news. Then I saw the dreadful article. The Luxembourg Gardens were going to be amputated of ten hectares in order to ameliorate the traffic on the rue Bonaparte and the rue Férou. The lovely tree nursery on the southern part of the gardens was to be whittled away for the same reasons. I leaped to my feet, startling Germaine, and rushed downstairs to the flower shop. Alexandrine was waiting for an important delivery.

"Don't tell me you agree with the Prefect over this," I snarled, shoving the paper at her. I was so angry my feet fairly stamped the floor. She read the article hurriedly and her mouth pulled down. She was, after all, an ardent nature lover. "Oh," she exclaimed, "what a terrible thing to do!"

That afternoon, in spite of the cold, people gathered in front of the garden gates on the top of the rue Férou. I went along with Alexandrine and Monsieur Zamaretti. There was soon quite a crowd, and the gendarmes were called to keep everything in control. Students shouted, "Long live the Luxembourg Gardens!" as petitions went around feverishly. I must have signed three, with a clumsy, gloved hand. It was exciting seeing how all these different Parisians, from all ages, all classes, were coming together to protect their gardens. An elegant lady next to me was deep in conversation with a shopkeeper. Madame Paccard was with all her staff from the hotel. Mademoiselle Vazembert had two gentlemen on each arm. And from afar, I saw the adorable Baronne de Vresse and her husband, with the governess and the little girls in tow.

The rue de Vaugirard was now black with people. I wondered how on earth we were all going to get home, but it did not bother me. I felt safe with Alexandrine and Monsieur Zamaretti. All of us here, each and every one, stood united against the Prefect. It felt marvelous. He would hear about us the next morning, when he scanned all the papers for his name, with his team, which is apparently his first daily action. He would hear about us when the petitions started to pile on his desk. How dare he amputate our magical gardens! All of us there that afternoon shared special ties to this place, to the palace, the fountains, the grand bassin, the statues, the flower beds. This peaceful garden was the symbol of our childhood, of our memories. We had put up with the Prefect's overzealous ambitions long enough. We would stand up to him this time. We would not let him tamper with the Luxembourg Gardens.

For several days we all met there, with even more protesters each time. You would have found it thrilling. The petitions grew thicker and the articles in the newspapers were most negative regarding the Prefect. Students started to riot, and one evening the Emperor himself was confronted with the crowds as he was about to attend a play at the Odéon Theater. I was not there that time, but I heard about it from Alexandrine. She told me the Emperor seemed embarrassed, pausing on the steps, ensconced in his cloak. He listened to what was being said and he gravely nodded his head.

A few weeks later, Alexandrine and I read that the decree was being amended because the Emperor had ordered the Prefect to revise his plans. We felt elated. Alas, our happiness was short-lived. The gardens were indeed to be truncated, but not as severely as at first. However, the tree nursery was doomed. It was a disappointing victory. And then, just as the Luxembourg affair died down, an even more hideous one sprouted up. I cannot even begin to choose the proper words to describe it to you.

Believe it or not, the Prefect had become

obsessed with the business of death. He was convinced the dust in the Parisian cemeteries emanating from the rotting of corpses was contaminating the water. I read with shock in the paper that the Prefect envisaged closing down the graveyards within the city for sanitation reasons. The dead were now to be taken to Méry-sur-Oise, near Pontoise, thirty kilometers away, to a huge graveyard, a modern necropolis. The Prefect had imagined special death trains departing from all Parisian stations, in which families could travel with their dead one's coffin for burial at Méry. This was such a monstrous thing to read that at first I could not go down to show it to Alexandrine. I simply could not move. I thought of my loved ones, you and Baptiste and Maman Odette. I imagined taking a sinister train swathed in black crepe, full of mourners, undertakers and priests, in order to visit your graves. I felt as if I was going to burst into tears. I believe I did. In fact, I did not have to show the paper to Alexandrine. She had already read about it. But this time she thought the Prefect was right. She believed in the complete modernization of the water system, and thought it was a healthy idea to bury the dead out of the city limits. I was too upset to contradict her. Where were her own dead? I wondered. Not in Paris. If they had been, she would not have had this reaction.

Most people, however, were like me, scandalized. Even more so when the Prefect announced that the Montmartre Cemetery was to undergo transformations. Dozens of tombs were actually to be moved so that the pillars of a new bridge going over the hill could be built. The polemic raged. The papers were full of it. All the Prefect's opponents gave full vent to their venom. Monsieur Fournel and Monsieur Veuillot wrote brilliant, scathing pamphlets that you would have admired. After having sent thousands of Parisians packing and destroying their homes, he was now deporting the dead. Sacrilege! All of Paris was in an uproar. One could feel the Prefect tottering on very thin ice.

The coup de grâce came with the publication of a very moving article in the *Figaro*. A lady named Madame Audouard (one of those modern ladies who writes in a bold fashion, not like the Comtesse de Ségur and her mild tales for children) happened to have a son buried at Montmartre. I do not know how old that son was, but she and I shared the same wordless grief. When I read her article, I must admit I cried again. Her words are engraved in my heart forever. "Monsieur the Prefect, all nations, even those we call barbarians, respect the dead."

This time, Armand, the Emperor did not back up his Prefect. The opposition was so ferocious that the project was abandoned after a couple of months. The Prefect was now under attack, and fragile, for the first time. At last.

Sens, October 23rd, 1868
Dearest Madame Rose,

I cannot thank you enough for your invaluable support. I think you are the only person on this earth to veritably understand the turmoil and despair I endured when I had to accept that the hotel was to be destroyed. You and I know the power of houses, how they hold us in that power and how we revel in it. The hotel was like another part of me. I gave myself heart, body and soul to that building, and so did my beloved husband, when he was still with us. I remember the first time I laid eyes on the hotel. It was a dark and sullen form crouching by the church. No one had lived in it for years, it was swarming with mice and reeked of humidity.

Gaston, my husband, immediately saw what could be done with it. Yes, he had the eye, as they say. Sometimes houses are like people, they are shy, they do not give their personalities away that easily. It took a while to conquer that house, to tame it, to call it ours, but we did it and each moment was a moment of joy.

I knew from the start I wanted a hotel. I knew what that entailed, what an enormous amount of work it meant, but I was not daunted, and neither was Gaston. When they hung the sign up for the first time, "Hôtel Belfort," on the first-floor balcony, I could have swooned with joy and pride. As you know, the hotel was nearly always fully booked. It was the only good establishment within the area, and once word of mouth started, we were never short of clients.

Madame Rose, how I miss my clients, their chatter, their fidelity, their whims. Even the odd ones. Even the respectable gentlemen who took young lasses up for a quick tumble when I looked the other way. Do you remember Monsieur and Madame Roche, who came every June for their wedding anniversary? And Mademoiselle Brunerie, the charming old maid, who always reserved the room on the top floor, the one that gave on to the church's roof? She said it made her feel closer to God. I sometimes wonder how it is possible that a place in which I felt so secure, which I called home, but which was also how I earned money, which brought us our income, could be so easily erased from the face of the earth.

As you know, I chose to leave before the rue Childebert was demolished. I am now writing to you from my sister's house in Sens, where I am trying to set up a pension de famille, and not being very successful about it. I remember how we fought till the bitter end, especially you, I and Docteur Nonant. It seemed to me that the other inhabitants of the street accepted their fate with ease. Perhaps they had less to lose. Perhaps they even looked forward to starting a new life elsewhere. I sometimes wonder what they have all become.

I know we will probably never see our neighbors again. Such an odd thought, as every single morning of our lives we would greet each other. All those familiar faces, those familiar buildings and shops. Monsieur Jubert admonishing his team, Monsieur Horace already pink-nosed at nine in the morning, Madame Godfin and Mademoiselle Vazembert at it like a pair of squabbling hens, Monsieur Bougrelle chatting with Monsieur Zamaretti, and the rich, marvelous chocolate smell wafting from

Monsieur Monthier's boutique. I have lived so very many years in the rue Childebert, perhaps forty, nay, forty-five, and I cannot envisage that the street no longer exists. I do not want to lay eyes on the modern boulevard that swallowed it up. Ever.

Have you decided to move to your daughter's home, Madame Rose? Please give me some news from time to time. Should you care to visit me here in Sens, let me know. The town is pleasant enough. A welcome rest from the endless works, dust and noise of Paris. I take comfort in the fact that my clients still write to me and tell me how much they miss the hotel. You know how I pampered them. Each room was spotless, decorated with simplicity and good taste, and Mademoiselle Alexandrine delivered fresh flowers every day, not to mention the chocolates from Monsieur Monthier.

How I miss standing at the reception area and greeting my clients. Such an international crowd too. How maddening to have to close down in the middle of the Exposition Universelle. And how atrocious to have to accept the total destruction of so many years of work.

I think of you often, Madame Rose. Your grace and kindness to everyone on the street; your great courage when your husband passed away. He was such a gentleman, Monsieur Bazelet. I know he would have hated seeing his beloved home destroyed. I remember the two of you walking down the street, before his illness took over. What a fine pair you made. Gorgeous, good-looking and so charming, both of you. And I remember, Lord have mercy, the little boy. Madame Rose, no one will ever forget your little boy. God bless him and you. I hope you are happy with your daughter, I seem to recall you were not that close to her. Maybe this ordeal will bring you closer at last. I send you my friendship and my prayers and hope that we may meet again.

Micheline Paccard

My books, down here with me. Fine ones, beautifully bound, in all different colors. I do not wish to ever separate myself from them. *Madame Bovary,* of course, the one that opened the door to the bewitching world of reading. Baudelaire's *Les Fleurs du Mal,* which I pick up from time to time as the hours glide by. The fascinating aspect about poems, as opposed to novels, is that one can read just a couple, and a few more later on, like a sort of continuous treat that one nibbles at. Monsieur Baudelaire's poems are strange and haunting. They are full of images, sounds and colors, sometimes disturbing.

Would you have liked them? I suspect so. They play on one's nerves and senses. My favorite one is "The Perfume Flask." It is about scents harboring memories, and how a perfume can bring back one's past. I know the smell of roses will always remind me of

Alexandrine and the Baronne. Cologne water and talcum powder are you, my love. Hot milk and honey are Baptiste. Verbena and lavender are Maman Odette. Had you still been here, I would no doubt have read this poem to you, over and over again.

Sometimes reading a book leads one to another book. Did you not experience that? I am sure you did. I discovered that rather quickly. Monsieur Zamaretti let me roam about the rows in his shop. I even climbed up the ladder to reach up higher. You see, Armand, there was a new hunger within me, and on some days I can assure you I felt fairly ravenous. The need to read took over me, a delicious and exhilarating hold. The more I read, the hungrier I became. Each book seemed promising, each page I turned offered an escapade, the allure of another world, other destinies, other dreams. So what did I read? you may well ask.

Charles Baudelaire led me to an author, American I believe, named Edgar Allan Poe. How could I resist the fact that Monsieur Baudelaire himself had translated those stories? It gave the whole matter an added attraction. When my favorite poet died last year, I read he was buried in our very own cemetery, in Montparnasse. Yes, Charles Baudelaire's eternal resting place is just a couple of alleys away from you, Baptiste and Maman Odette. I have been too tired of late to go there, but the last time I went, I visited his tomb. There was a letter placed on his grave. It had been rained on, the ink had spread over the paper like a large black flower.

In Monsieur Poe's stories I found the same haunting, powerful themes that appealed to me so deeply. And I could see, so very clearly, why Monsieur Baudelaire had chosen to translate his work. They had the same scope, the same vision. Yes, you could say they were macabre, thick with mystery, lush with imagination. Are you perplexed by your mild Rose's astonishing literary tastes? The story I prefer is called "The Fall of the House of Usher." It takes place in a gloomy, ivy-covered mansion overlooking a dark and silent tarn. The narrator is summoned by an old friend undergoing a nameless illness and who needs his help. I cannot begin to describe what a thrill I experienced when I first read that story. I felt chills running up and down my spine. Such a climate of malevolence, of fear, of otherworldly forces contriving toward doom. At times I had to pause to catch my breath, at times I felt I could not go on reading, that this stuff was too strong a potion, that it would overcome me. I could not breathe. And yet, I had to rush back to the page, no one and nothing could tear me away from Roderick Usher's ghastly secret, from the spectral apparition of Madeline in her blood-stained dress, from the entire mansion crumbling into the tarn. Monsieur Poe knew how to wield his magic.

This morning the noises have taken up again, despite the prevailing cold. It will not be long now. I do not have much time, so I will resume my story. There is so much I need to tell you, still. Six months ago, Madame Paccard, Docteur Nonant and myself decided to go to the Hôtel de Ville to protest against the destruction of our street. Our numerous letters had been answered by office clerks who, as you can imagine, merely repeated that the decision was irrevocable, but that one could expect to negotiate the sum of money that was being allotted to us. But for the three of us, money was not the issue. We wanted to keep our premises.

So you must imagine the three of us, on that June day. Most determined we were, Madame Paccard and her quivering bun, Docteur Nonant with his grave whiskered face, and your Rose, in her best claret-colored silk coat and a veiled bonnet. We crossed the river on a clear warm morning, and I was impressed, as always, by the formidable Renaissance-style building that awaited us on the other side of the bridge. Nervousness clenched at my stomach and I felt almost dizzy with anticipation as we neared the huge stone façade. Were we not mad to envisage even one instant that we would see the man himself? And would he ever listen to us? I was relieved not to be alone, to have my two companions by my side. They appeared much more assured than I did.

In the enormous entrance, in which I had never been, I noticed a fountain tinkling under wide, circling stairs. Clusters of people were ambling about the great hall, awed by the ornate ceilings, the grandeur of the place. So this was where he lived and worked, him, that man, whose name I still cannot bring myself to write. He and his family (that mouselike wife, Octavie, who apparently loathes mundane life, those two daughters, Henriette and Valentine, pink, buxom and golden-haired, trussed up like prize cows) slept under this tremendous roof, somewhere in the labyrinthine recesses of this grandiose place.

Oh, we had read in the papers all about

the sumptuous, lavish parties held here, with such pomp that one would think he were the Sun King himself. Baronne de Vresse had been to the party thrown for the Tsar and the King of Prussia a year ago, with three orchestras and a thousand guests. She had also attended the reception in honor of Franz Josef of Austria the following October, with four hundred guests served by three hundred footmen. She had described the seven-course meal, the vast amounts of flowers, the crystal glasses and fine porcelain, the fifty giant candelabras. The Empress wore a taffeta dress fringed with rubies and diamonds. (Alexandrine gaped at this, and I had remained stonily silent.) All Parisians knew about the Prefect's wine cellar, the finest in the city. All Parisians knew that if one passed by the rue de Rivoli in the early hours, the only light to be seen burning in a single window of the Hôtel de Ville would be that of the Prefect, slaving away only in order to dispatch his army of pickaxes over our city.

As we did not have a rendezvous with anyone in particular, we were told to make our way to the first floor, to the Bureau of Domains and Expropriations. When we got there, we saw with sinking hearts a long line of people also waiting. We took our turn in the queue, as patiently as possible. I wondered who all these people were and what sort of claims they were going to make. The lady next to me was my age, with a weary face and untidy clothes. But the rings on her fingers were fine and precious. By her side was a bearded man, unsmiling and impatient, tapping his feet, staring at his watch every ten minutes. There was also a family, two young parents, very proper, with a fretful baby and a bored little girl.

Everyone waited. From time to time a door would open and a clerk would come to take down the names of the new arrivals. I felt it would last forever. When our turn finally came, we were not allowed to go in together, but one by one. No wonder the whole matter took so long! We let Madame Paccard go first.

The minutes dragged by. When she came out at last, her face seemed to have sagged even more. She muttered something I did not catch and sank down into her seat, her head in her hands. Docteur Nonant and I watched anxiously. The lady with the rumpled clothes then also emerged in the same state, tears running down her face. I began to feel most nervous. I let Docteur Nonant go before me, as I felt I needed to stretch my legs for a while. The room felt stuffy and clammy, full of other people's smell and anguish.

I went outside into the large corridor and paced up and down. The place was a beehive of activity. It was here that it all happened, you see. The slow destruction of our city was born here. All the busy men rushing around with papers and folders had something to do with the work. Which of them had decided that the boulevard would pass just by the church, which of them had sketched the actual plans, which of them had drawn the first lethal line?

We had read all about the Prefect's splendid team. We knew their faces, as they had each become famous. The crème de la crème of the intelligentsia of our country, all brilliant engineers with the highest diplomas, from Polytechnique, from the Ponts and Chaussées. Monsieur Victor Baltard, the "iron man," builder of the gigantic marketplace I was telling you about. Monsieur Jean-Charles Alphand, the "gardener," famed for giving our city its new lungs. Monsieur Eugène Belgrand, the notorious "water man," obsessed with our sewers. Monsieur Gabriel Davioud, who designed the two theaters on the place du Châtelet, but also that unfortunate, oversized fountain at Saint-Michel. Each of these gentlemen had his grandiose role to play, basking in the glory.

And the Emperor, of course, watching it all from the high golden haven of his palaces, far from the rubble, the dust, the tragedy.

When I was at last called in, I found myself sitting in front of a fair young man who could have been my grandson. He had long wavy hair that he seemed inordinately proud of, an immaculate dark suit of the latest fashion and shiny shoes. His face was smooth, with the delicate complexion of a young girl. His desk was piled high with files and binders. Behind him an older bespectacled gentleman scribbled away, huddled over his work. The young man flickered lazy, arrogant eyes over me, glancing at his watch. He lit a small cigar, puffed away importantly and then asked me to voice my complaint. I replied calmly that I was firmly opposed to the destruction of my family home. He asked me for my name and address, opened a thick book, slid a finger down a couple of pages. Then he muttered:

"Cadoux, Rose, widow of Armand Bazelet, six rue Childebert."

"Yes, monsieur," I said, "that is I."

"You do not agree with the sum of money proposed by the Préfecture, I presume?"

He said this with boredom, tinged with despicable nonchalance, glancing at his nails as he spoke. How old was this arrogant brat? I thought, seething. No doubt he had other, more pleasurable topics on his mind, a luncheon with a young lady, or a gala evening tonight. What suit should he wear? The brown, the blue? And would he have time to have his hair curled before nightfall? I said nothing as I sat there in front of him, one hand laid out flat on the desk that separated us.

When he finally looked up at me, probably surprised at my silence, a guarded expression filtered into his eyes. I could tell he was thinking: This one is going to make a fuss, I will be late for my lunch. I could see myself in his gaze, one of those respectable old ladies, well turned out, probably quite a looker in her day, centuries ago, and now here to demand more money. They all did that. Sometimes they ended up getting more money. So he thought.

"What is the sum you are considering, Madame Bazelet?"

"I do not think you have fully grasped the nature of my purpose, monsieur."

He stiffened, raising an eyebrow.

"And, pray, what is the purpose you have in mind, madame?"

239

Oh, the irony in his voice, the mockery. I could have slapped his smooth, round face.

I said, very clearly:

"I am opposed to the destruction of my family home."

He stifled a yawn.

"Yes, madame, I have gathered that."

"I do not want money," I said.

He seemed baffled.

"Then what is it you do want, madame?"

I took a deep breath.

"I want the Prefect to build the boulevard Saint-Germain farther away. I want to save my house and the rue Childebert."

His jaw dropped. He stared at me. Then his laugh burst out, an ugly, gurgling sound. Oh, how I hated him. He laughed and laughed, and the toadfish gentleman behind him laughed as well, until a door opened and some other man looked in, and joined in too, holding his sides, when the young rascal choked, "Madame wants the Prefect to move the boulevard in order to save her house." Doubled over, they cackled away merrily, pointing at me.

There was nothing more to be said or done. I got up, as dignified as I possibly could, and made my way out. In the adjoining room, Docteur Nonant was mopping his sweaty brow with his kerchief. When he saw my face, he shook his head and raised his palms in despair. Madame Paccard patted my arm. Of course, they had heard the laughs. The entire Hôtel de Ville had heard the laughs.

There were even more people in the room and the air was stifling and stale. We left in haste. And then suddenly we saw him, as we made our way down the stairs.

The Prefect. Towering over each and every person there, quite close to us, so near, in fact, that we drew breath and stopped short. I had seen him before, as I told you, but never from so close. There he was, at arm's reach. I could see the grain of his skin, slightly speckled, a florid hue, the curly harshness of his beard, the blaze of icy blue eyes. He was sturdy, running to fat, with hands like hams, formidable.

We flattened ourselves against the banister as he swept past, two or three clerks in his wake. He smelled of rancid sweat, liquor and tobacco. He did not see us. He seemed intent, implacable. I itched to reach out and grab his meaty wrist, to force him to look at me, to free my hatred, my fear, my anguish, to scream at him that by destroying my home he was destroying my memories, my life, the very core of it. But my hand remained limply by my side. And then he was gone.

We left in silence, the three of us. We had lost our battle. We had not dared speak to the Prefect, none of us had dared. There was nothing more to be done. The rue Childebert was doomed. The doctor would lose his patients; Madame Paccard, her hotel; and I, our house. We had no more hope. It was finished.

It was balmy outside, almost too hot. I secured my bonnet around my head as we crossed the bridge. I saw nothing of the activity on the river, with barges and boats gliding up and down, nor did I pay any heed to the traffic around us charged with top-heavy omnibuses and busy cabbies. I could still hear the jarring laughter and my cheeks smarted.

When I got back home, my dear, I was so incensed that I sat down at my desk and I wrote a long letter to the Prefect. I ordered Germaine to go to the post office to send it off immediately. I have no idea if he ever read it. But writing it did me good. It took some of the weight off my chest. I remember that letter perfectly well. After all, I wrote it not that long ago, did I not?

Sir,

You will no doubt never read this. But my letter may find its way into your hands. It is a slim chance I will take.

You do not know me. And you never will. My name is Rose Bazelet, née Cadoux, and I live on the rue Childebert, which is about to be flattened for the continuation of the rue de Rennes and the boulevard Saint-Germain.

For the past fifteen years I have endured you. I have endured your works, your avidity, your obduracy. I have endured the dust, the discomfort, the torrents of mud, the debris, the destructions and the advent of a tawdry, tinsel-like Paris which perfectly embodies the commonness of your purpose. I have endured the mutilation of the Luxembourg Gardens. Today, I have had enough.

This very day, sir, I went to the Hôtel de

243

Ville, like many other Parisians in my situation, in order to protest against the demolition of my family home. I do not care to relate the arrogance with which I was received.

Are you aware, sir, that there are citizens in this town who do not approve of your actions, nor the way with which these actions are taking place? Are you aware that you are called the "Attila of the straight line," the "Ripper Baron"? Perhaps these nicknames make you smile. Perhaps the Emperor and yourself have decided not to bother with what the populace thinks of your embellishments. Thousands of houses have been destroyed. Thousands of people have been forced to move, have been sent packing. Of course, as you are safely shielded in the preserved magnificence of the Hôtel de Ville, these discomforts mean little to you. And to you they are above all material. You are convinced that a family home is simply worth a sum of money. For you, a house is only a house. Your name is ironic. How is it possible that you are called "Haussmann"? Haussmann means "the man of the house" in German, does it not? I read that when you were building the continuation of the boulevard that now bears your name, you did not hesitate to raze the very house you were born in. I find that tells it all.

I am relieved to read in the press that you have a growing number of enemies, especially since the deplorable affair of the cemeteries. People are now questioning the impact that the complete reshaping of our capital will have in the future. These irrevocable transformations have tampered with communities, with neighborhoods, with families, and have annihilated even memory. The poorest citizens have been sent to live outside the city limits because they can no longer afford the rents of those new, modern buildings. All this will no doubt affect Parisians for very many years.

The damage is done. I no longer walk through the streets of my city, sir, because my city has become a foreign place to me.

I was born in this city, nearly sixty years ago, as you were. When you were appointed, I witnessed the beginnings of the transformations, I witnessed the enthusiasm, the appeal of modernity that was on everyone's lips. I saw the continuation of the rue de Rivoli, the opening of boulevard Sébastopol that ruined my brother's house, the opening of boulevard du Prince Eugène, the boulevard Magenta, the rue Lafayette, the rue Réaumur, the rue de Rennes, the boulevard Saint-Germain . . . I will not be here to witness the rest of your works, and of that I am immensely relieved.

I have one final comment to make. Have you not, the Emperor and yourself, been overwhelmed with the sheer grandiloquence of your project?

It appears that the enormity of your mutual ambitions has somehow led you to envisage that Paris is not only the capital of France, but of the entire world.

I will not bow down to you, sir. I will not bow down to the Emperor. I will not be sent away like the sheeplike Parisians whose entire existences you have dismantled. I will resist you, sir.

In the name of my late husband, Armand Bazelet, who was born, who lived, who loved and who died in our house rue Childebert, I shall never surrender.

Rose Bazelet

In the dead of the night, I felt a presence next to me and I nearly swooned. I thought for a few panic-stricken seconds that it was the intruder and that no one would ever hear me screaming down here in the cellar. I thought my last hour had come. For agonizing moments, I fumbled with matches to light my candle.

I called out in a quavering voice, "Who is there?"

A warm hand found its way to mine. To my relief and amazement, it was Alexandrine. She had entered the house with her old key, had crept down the stairs in the dark to me. She had at last understood I was hiding here. I begged her not to reveal my presence to anyone. She kept staring at me in the dim candlelight. She appeared most agitated.

"You have been here all this time, Madame Rose?"

I explained carefully that I had been helped by Gilbert, my ragpicker friend, that he brought me food, water and coal daily and that I was perfectly all right despite the freezing cold that had besieged the city. She seized my hand, fairly stuttering with emotion as she cried out, "Oh, but you cannot stay here any longer, Madame Rose! The house will be pulled down in the next twenty-four hours! It would be madness to stay, you will . . ." Her eyes met mine, those toffee-colored eyes shining with intelligence, and I looked back at her, calmly, my back straight. She seemed to be searching for an answer deep inside me, and I gave her that answer, speechlessly. She dissolved into tears. I gathered her into my arms and we stayed that way for a long while, until her sobs abated somewhat. When she seemed to have regained her composure, she merely whispered, "Why?"

The vastness of her question engulfed me. How could I possibly explain? Where would I begin? The sharp, cold silence drew itself around us. It seemed I had been living down here forever, that I would never again glimpse the light of day. What time was it? It did not matter. The night appeared to be standing still. The musty smell of the cellar had weaved its way into Alexandrine's hair, her clothes.

She felt like a daughter as I clutched her against me, as if we were made of the same flesh, the same blood. We shared warmth, and some sort of love, I suppose, a powerful bond of affection that linked her to me, and I felt closer to her at that moment than I had ever felt with anyone in my life, even with you. I sensed I could tell her all my burdens. I felt she could understand. I took a deep breath. I began by telling her that this house was all my life, that each room told a story, my story, your story. Since you had left, I had never found a way to replace your absence. Your illness had not made my love for you any weaker, on the contrary.

The house bore the story of our love in its inner structure, in its quaint beauty. The house was my link to you, forever. By losing the house, I would again lose you.

"I used to think this house would live on forever," I whispered to Alexandrine in the dark heart of the night, "that it would go on standing, impervious to time, to battles, to events, like the church still stands today. I thought this house would live on after Armand, after me, that there would be other little boys who would one day tear down the stairs, laughing, other slender dark girls to curl up on the sofa near the fire, other gentlemen who would calmly read by the window. I believed the house would witness other family sorrows, joys and tragedies. When I looked ahead, or when I tried to, I always saw the house, its stability. It appeared immutable. Year after year, I believed it would keep the same familiar odor, the same cracks on the wall, the creak of the stairs, the uneven flagstones in the kitchen, the way the sun would shine inside, depending on the seasons. I was wrong. The house is doomed. And never will I abandon it."

Alexandrine listened very quietly, not once interrupting me. I lost track of time, and my voice droned on through the dimness, like a strange beacon taking us to day, to dawn. I think maybe she fell asleep after a while, and so did I.

When I opened my eyes, I knew Gilbert was there, I could hear him rummaging upstairs as the smell of coffee floated down to us. Alexandrine stirred and mumbled a few words. I gently brushed her hair away from her face. She looked so young as she lay there in my arms, her skin fresh and rosy. I wondered why no man had ever found a way to her heart. I wondered what her life was like, apart from the flowers that were essential to her existence. Was she lonely? She was such a creature of mystery.

When she awoke at last, I could tell she was having trouble remembering where she was. She could not believe she had slept down here with me. I led her upstairs, where Gilbert had prepared coffee. She looked at him, nodded her head. Then her face sobered when she recalled our conversation during the night. She took my hand and held it tight, with a pleading, yearning expression. But I remained firm. I shook my head.

All of a sudden her face turned beetroot-red and she grabbed me by the shoulders and started to shake me furiously.

"You cannot do this! You cannot do this, Madame Rose!"

She yelled this at the top of her voice, tears streaming down her cheeks. I tried to calm her down, but she would not listen, her features contorted, unrecognizable. She had worked herself into a proper state. Gilbert leaped up, spilling coffee over the floor, and firmly plucked her away from me.

"What about those who care for you, who need you?" she hissed, heaving, struggling to break free, pushing and kicking. "What am I going to do without you, Madame Rose? How can you leave me like this, don't you see how selfish you are? I need you, Madame Rose. I need you like flowers need

251

the rain. You are so very precious to me. Don't you see?"

Her sorrow touched me deeply. Never had I seen her act this way. For ten years Alexandrine had come across as a composed person, full of authority. She knew how to make herself respected. Nobody ever got the better of her. And here she was, sobbing, her face devastated with grief, her hands outstretched to me. How could I do this, she went on, how could I be so cruel, so heartless? Had I not understood that I was like a mother to her, that I was her best friend, her only friend?

I listened. I listened and I cried as well, silently, not daring to look at her any longer. The tears ran down my face unchecked.

"You could come and live with me," she whispered, exhausted now, her voice a mere croak. "I would look after you, I would be there to protect you, you know I would do that for you, Madame Rose. You would never be alone. You would never be alone again."

Gilbert's deep voice boomed out, startling us both.

"That will be enough, mademoiselle," he announced. She turned to glare at him. He looked down at her, amused, stroking his black beard. "Madame Rose is looked after by me. She is not alone."

Alexandrine tossed her head contemptuously. I was glad to see that some spirit had returned.

"You?" she scoffed.

"Yes, I," he retorted, rather grandly, stretching himself up to his full height.

"But surely, monsieur, you agree that Madame Rose's plan to stay in the house till the end is pure madness."

He shrugged, as he always did.

"That is Madame Rose's decision. And hers alone."

"If that is what you think, monsieur, then I believe we do not share the same feelings for Madame Rose."

He seized her arm, looming menacingly above her.

"What do you know about feelings?" he spat. "Mademoiselle who's always slept in a clean bed, who's never gone hungry, proper Mademoiselle with her fine nose stuck in flower petals. What do you know about love and pain and sorrow? What do you know about life and death? Tell me!"

"Oh, let me go," she moaned, shaking him off. She stepped to the other side of the bare kitchen and turned her back to us.

There was a long silence. I watched them both, these two odd creatures who had taken up such an important space in my life in these last years. I knew nothing of their past, of their secrets, and yet it seemed to me that they were strangely alike in their loneliness, their stance, their garb. Tall, thin, wrapped in black, pale faces, tangled dark hair. The same glare in their bright eyes. The same hidden wounds. Where did Gilbert get that limp? Where was he born, who was his family, what was his story? Why was Alexandrine always alone? Why did she never talk about herself? I would no doubt never know.

I held out a hand to each of them. Their palms were cold and dry in mine.

"Please do not fight over me," I said very calmly. "You both mean so much to me in these last moments."

They nodded wordlessly, their eyes not meeting mine.

The day had risen now, pale white and brilliant, icy cold. To my surprise, Gilbert handed me the greatcoat and fur hat I had worn the night he took me out to see the neighborhood.

"Put this on, Madame Rose. And you, mademoiselle, fetch your coat. Wrap up warm."

"Where are we going?" I asked, startled.

"Not far. Only for an hour or so. We must go quick. Trust me. You will like it. You too, mademoiselle."

Alexandrine meekly did as she was told. I believe she was too tired and too upset to put up another fight.

Outside, the sun shone like a strange jewel, hanging low in the sky, almost white. The cold was so intense that I could feel it cutting through my lungs every time I drew breath. I could not bear seeing the partially destroyed rue Childebert once more, so I kept my eyes down. He hurried us up the rue Bonaparte, limping badly. The street was deserted. I did not see a living soul, not even a hackney. The pale light, the freezing air, seemed to have stifled all life. Where was he taking us? We rushed onwards, my arm tucked under Alexandrine's. She was shivering from head to toe.

We reached the riverside, and there was the most astounding sight. Remember that bitterly cold winter just before Violette was born, when we had come to this place between the Pont des Arts and the Pont Neuf, to watch enormous blocks of ice roll by? This time, the cold was so severe that the entire river had iced over. Gilbert led us down to the docks, where a couple of barges trapped by the ice did not budge. I hesitated, I pulled back, but Gilbert said to trust him. So I did.

The river was covered with a thick, uneven gray crust. As far as I could see, looking up toward the Ile de la Cité, people were walking on the Seine. A dog pranced madly up and down, jumping and barking and sometimes slipping. Gilbert urged me to be very careful. Alexandrine ran on ahead, ecstatic, like a child, whooping. We reached the middle of the river. I could glimpse brown water churning beneath the ice. Loud cracks could be heard from time to time. They startled me. Again Gilbert told me not to be afraid. It was so cold there was at least one meter of ice, he said.

How I longed for you at that moment, Armand. How you would have been thunderstruck by this astonishing sight. It was like being in another world. I watched Alexandrine cavort with the little black dog. The sun rose slowly, as pale as ever, and more and more people came down to the river. The minutes seemed to stand still, like the frozen layer beneath my feet. The clamor of voices and laughter. The crisp, icy breeze. The shriek of gulls in the air.

I knew, as I stood there, with Gilbert's comforting arm around me, that my time had come. I knew the end loomed up ahead and that the choice was mine. I could still back away, I could still leave the house. But

I was not afraid. Gilbert glanced down at me as I stood silently by his side and I could tell he knew exactly what I was thinking.

And I recalled the last meal that Monsieur Helder had given in his restaurant on the rue Erfurth. All the neighbors had attended. Yes, we were all there, Monsieur and Madame Barou, Alexandrine, Monsieur Zamaretti, Docteur Nonant, Monsieur Jubert, Madame Godfin, Mademoiselle Vazembert, Madame Paccard, Monsieur Horace, Monsieur Bougrelle, Monsieur Monthier. We sat at those long narrow tables you liked so much, beneath the brass hat racks and next to the walls yellowed with smoke. The lace-curtained windows gave on to the rue Childebert and part of the rue Erfurth. We had lunched and dined there so many times. You had a soft spot for the salé aux lentilles, I enjoyed the bavette. I sat there, between Madame Barou and Alexandrine, and I simply could not take in that in a couple of weeks or months all this would be gone, wiped away, eradicated. We had a solemn meal. No one talked much. Even Monsieur Horace's jokes fell flat. As we ate our desserts, Monsieur Helder spotted Gilbert hobbling down the street. He knew we were friends. He opened the door and gruffly invited Gilbert in. Nobody seemed to mind the presence of a tattered ragpicker amidst us. Gilbert sat down, nodding his head respectfully to everyone, and managed to eat his meringue with a certain amount of grace, I thought. His eyes met mine and they twinkled merrily. Oh, he must have been a good-looking lad, once. At the end of the lunch, while we were having coffee, Monsieur Helder gave an awkward speech. He wished to thank each and every one of us for being his customers. He was off now to Corrèze, where his wife and he would open up a new restaurant near Brive-la-Gaillarde, where his wife's family lived. They did not want to stay in a city that was being so heavily modernized and that was, they felt, they feared, losing its soul. Paris had become another Paris, he deplored, and as long as he still had energy within him, then he would take that energy elsewhere and start over.

It was that day, after that last, tearful meal at Chez Paulette, that I found myself walking down the street with Gilbert by my side. His was a comforting presence. The entire street had started to pack up and move away. Carts and hackneys were parked in front of each house. The movers were coming to fetch my furniture early next week. Gilbert asked me where I was going to go.

Until then, my response to that question had invariably been: I am going to my daughter Violette's place, near Tours. But somehow I knew that with this odd stranger I could be myself. No need to lie.

And so you see, dearest, I said to him that day: "I am not leaving. I shall never leave my house." He seemed to understand what this entailed perfectly. He nodded. He did not even question me. The only thing he added, a few minutes later, was this:

"I am here to help you, Madame Rose. I will help you in any way."

I looked up at him and searched his face.

"And why would you do that, pray?"

He paused, long, grimy fingers stroking the length of his tangled beard.

"You are a rare, precious person, Madame Rose. You have always helped me out these past years. Life has not been kind. I lost my loved ones. I have lost all my belongings, my home, and even most of my hope. But when I am with you, I feel there is still some hope left. A glimmer of hope. Even in this modern, tiring world that I don't understand."

That was undoubtedly the longest speech he had ever uttered in my presence. I was moved, as you can imagine, and I struggled to find appropriate words. They did not come. So I merely patted his sleeve. He nodded his head, he smiled. There was a mixture of sadness and joy in his eyes. I wanted to question him about his loved ones, about his losses. But between him and I flowed an undercurrent of understanding and respect. We did not need to ask each other questions. We did not need answers.

I knew then that I had found the one person who would never judge me. The one person who would never stop me.

The work will take up again soon, Gilbert announced, as he accompanied me back to the house. We walked slowly, as the streets were still crisp with ice. Alexandrine had left when we were still on the river. She had not said good-bye. She had not looked at me once. I watched her walk away, heading north, her back very stiff and straight. I could tell how angry she still was with me just by the way her arms swung in a tight, menacing way. Would she be back? Would she try to stop me? What would I do if she did?

We spotted a group of workers by the end of the rue Erfurth, or rather, what was left of it, and Gilbert had to use both cunning and caution to get us back to the house. He has gone out now to get food, and I am sitting in my hiding place, still wearing the heavy, warm coat.

I do not have much time now. I will begin

to tell you what you need to know. This is not easy. So I will keep my words simple. As simple as I can. Forgive me.

I never knew what his full name was. He was merely called Monsieur Vincent and I am not certain whether that was his first name or his last. You no doubt do not recall him. To you he was insignificant. When this happened, I was thirty years old. Maman Odette had been gone for three years. Violette was nearly eight.

The first time I saw him was by the water fountain, one morning as I was walking with our daughter. I noticed him simply because he was staring at me. He was sitting by the fountain with a group of men I did not know, a thickset, freckled fellow, with short fair hair and a square jaw. He was younger than me. He liked to give the ladies the eye, I understood that fairly soon. There was something vulgar about him, his clothes, maybe, or his demeanor.

I did not like him from the start. There was an untrustworthy expression in his eyes, a false smile that seemed to stretch his face. "Oh, he's a ladies' man," murmured Madame Chanteloup over your starched chemises. "Who?" I asked, just to be sure. "That young fellow, that Monsieur Vincent. The new one working with Monsieur Jubert." Every time I set foot from the house, to go to the market, to take my daughter to her piano lessons, to visit Maman Odette's grave, there he was, lurking on the threshold of the printing house, as if he had been waiting. I was sure he was looking out for me. He did this in a predatory fashion that unnerved me. I never felt at ease in his company. His glittering eyes had a way of boring into mine.

What did he want, this young man? Why was he waiting for me, every morning, just to say a couple of words? What did he expect? At first he upset me to such an extent that I shied away from him. When I saw his silhouette etched out in front of the building, I ran, head down, as if I had urgent business to attend to. I even remember telling you how much this young man annoyed me, trying to spark off a conversation. You laughed. You thought it was flattering, this youngster, harping after your wife. That means my Rose is still fresh, my Rose is still lovely, you said, fondly kissing the top of my head. I did not find that amusing. Could you not have been a little more jealous? I would have enjoyed a spurt of envy. Monsieur Vincent changed his attitude when he understood I was not going to talk back to him. He became extremely polite, almost deferent. He rushed to help me with my shopping, my parcels, or if I happened to alight from a hackney. He became positively agreeable.

Little by little, my distrust faded. His charm operated, slowly but surely. I became accustomed to his warmth, his greetings. And I began to look out for them. Oh, dearest, how vain we women are. How foolish. There I was, ridiculously basking in this young man's constant attention. If one day I had not caught a glance of him, I wondered where he was. And when I did behold him, a blush invaded my face. Yes, he had a way with women. And I should have known better.

The day this happened, you were away. Somehow he knew that. You had left to visit a property with your notary, out of the city. You would not be back till the following day. Germaine and Mariette were not yet at our service. A girl came in and when she left at the end of the day I was alone with Violette.

He knocked that evening just as I had finished my solitary dinner. I looked down to the rue Childebert, my napkin to my lips, and I saw him standing there, his hat in his hands. I recoiled from the window. What on earth did he want? I did not go down to open up, however charming he had been of late. He finally went away and I believed I was safe. However, an hour or so later, when night had fallen, another knock was heard. I was about to go to bed. I was wearing my blue nightdress and my dressing gown. Our daughter was sleeping upstairs. The house was silent, dark. I went down. I did not open the door, I asked who was there.

" 'Tis me, Monsieur Vincent. I only want to talk to you, Madame Rose, just for a minute. Please open the door."

His voice sounded gentle and kind. The same kind voice he had been using with me for the past weeks. It fooled me. I opened up.

He swept in, too fast. There was a strong whiff of liquor on his breath. He looked down at me like an animal stares at its prey. Those glittering eyes. An icy fear seeped into my bones. And then I knew letting him in had been a terrible mistake. There was no small talk. He lunged out for me with those freckled hands, an ugly, greedy gesture, his fingers biting cruelly into my arms, his breath hot on my face. I managed to drag myself away with a sob, I managed to run up the stairs, a silent scream tearing my throat. But he was too quick. He caught me by the back of my neck as I entered the living room, and we tumbled down to the carpet, his loathsome hands at my breast, his wet mouth slippery on mine.

I tried to reason with him, I tried to tell him this was horribly wrong, that my daughter was in the upstairs room, that you were coming back, that he could not do this. He could not do this.

He was heedless. He did not listen. He did not care. He overpowered me. He crushed me to the ground. I feared my bones would break under his weight. I want you to understand there was nothing I could do. Nothing. I put up a fight. I fought him as hard as I could. I pulled his greasy hair, I writhed, I kicked, I bit, I spat. I could not bring myself to scream, because my daughter was just upstairs, and I could not bear her coming down to witness this. I wished above all to protect her.

When I realized that fighting was no good, I remained stonelike, a statue. I cried. I cried all the way through, dearest. I cried in silence. He had his way. I willed myself away from this hideous moment. I remember looking up at the ceiling and its slight cracks and waiting for this ordeal to end. I could smell the musty scent of the carpet, and his awful odor, the stink of a stranger, a stranger in my house, a stranger within my body. It happened very quickly, barely a couple of minutes, but to me it was a century. There was a ghastly leer on his face, his mouth was fully stretched out, turned up at the sides. Never will I forget that monstrous grin, the glistening of his teeth, the loll of his tongue.

He left without a word, sneering down at me, and I lay there like a corpse. I lay there for what seemed hours. Then I crept up and went to our room. I fetched water and I washed myself. The water was icy and I flinched. My skin was bruised and purple. I ached all over. I wanted to cower into a corner and shriek. I thought I would go mad. I felt filthy, contaminated.

The house was not safe. The house had been invaded. The house had been ravaged. I could almost feel the walls trembling. It had taken him five minutes. But the deed was done. The damage was done.

I did not sleep that night. His glittering eyes. His rapacious hands. That was when I had the nightmare for the first time. I went up to my daughter. She slept on, warm and drowsy. I lay there listening to her quiet breathing. I swore to myself I would never tell a living soul about this. Not even Père Levasque at confession. I could not even mention it in my most intimate prayers.

Who was there to tell, anyway? I was not close to my mother. I had no sister. My daughter was far too young. And I could not bring myself to speak of this to you. What would you have done? How would you have reacted? In my head I went back to the scene, again and again. Had I not egged him on? Had I not been inadvertently flirtatious? Was this not my fault? How could I have opened the door wearing my nightgown? I had not behaved decently. How could I have been duped by his voice through the door?

But wouldn't this appalling event have shamed you profoundly, had I ever told you? Would you not think I'd been having an affair, that I was his mistress? I could not bear the shame. I could not bear imagining the expression on your face. I could not bear the gossip, the chatter, walking down the rue Childebert, the rue Erfurth, with eyes on me, the knowing smiles, the nudges, the whispers.

No one would know. No one would ever know.

The next morning he was there, smoking, in front of the printing house. I feared I would not have the strength to walk out of the building. For a moment I lingered there, pretending to look for my keys in my purse. Then I managed to take a few steps onto the cobblestones. I looked up. He was facing me. There was a long scratch down his cheek. He stared right at me, blatantly, a swagger in his stance. He flickered a lazy tongue over his lower lip. I glanced away, my face crimson.

How I hated him at that instant. How I longed to pry his eyes out. How many men like him, on our streets, men of his kind who force themselves on women? How many women endure in silence because they feel guilty, because they are afraid? Men like him make silence their law. He knew I would never denounce him. He knew I would never tell you. He was right.

Wherever he is now, all these years later, I have not forgotten him. Thirty years have swept past, and although I have never laid eyes on him again, I would recognize him instantly. I wonder what he has become. What kind of old man he has turned into. I wonder if he has ever had any inkling of the havoc he wreaked in my life.

When you returned the following day, do you remember how I clasped you in my arms, how I kissed you? How I held on to you for dear life? That night you took me, and I felt it was the only way to erase the passage of the other man.

Monsieur Vincent disappeared from our neighborhood soon after. I have never slept soundly since.

This morning Gilbert is back with fresh warm bread and some roasted chicken wings. He keeps glancing at me as we eat. I ask him what the matter is.

"They are coming," he finally utters. "The cold has broken."

I remain silent.

"There is still time," he whispers.

"No," I say firmly. I wipe my greasy chin with my palm.

"Very well."

He stands up awkwardly and holds out his hand.

"What are you doing?" I ask.

"I am not going to stay here and watch this," he mutters.

To my dismay, tears spill out of his eyes. I cannot think of what to say. He pulls me to him, his arms wrapped around my back like two enormous gnarled branches. From very close, his stench is overwhelming. Then he steps away, embarrassed. He fumbles about in his pocket and hands me a withered flower. It is a small ivory rose.

"Should you change your mind . . ." he begins.

One last gaze down to me. I shake my head.

Then he is gone.

I am very calm, dearest. I am ready. I hear them now, the slow sure thunder of their approach, the voices, the clamor. I must hurry to tell you the end of my story. I believe you know now, I believe you have understood.

I have tucked Gilbert's rose into my corsage. My hand trembles as I write this, and it is not the cold, it is not the fear of the workers making their way here. It is the heaviness of the moment, of what I must unburden myself with at last.

The little boy was very small still. He could not yet walk. We were in the Luxembourg Gardens, with the nanny (I cannot recall her name, a sweet, placid creature) by the Medicis Fountain. It was a fine windy spring day, the garden was full of children, mothers, birds and flowers. You were not there, of that I am certain. I had a pretty hat, and the blue ribbon kept getting undone, streaming behind me in the blustery breeze. Oh, how Baptiste laughed.

When the wind tossed the hat right off my head, he fairly exploded with glee, his lips curled into a wide smile. There was a fleeting expression on his face. His mouth stretched out into a grin that I had already seen and that I had been unable to erase from my mind.

A hideous grin. It was a vision of awfulness that pierced through me like a dagger. I clutched a hand to my bosom and stifled a scream. Alarmed, the young nanny asked if I was all right. I steadied myself. My hat had gone, frolicking along the dusty path like a wild creature. Baptiste whimpered, pointing at it. I managed to get my composure back and staggered along to fetch it. But all along my heart thumped dreadfully. How could I not have expected such a tragedy? The extreme agitation I had experienced after the attack had forced me to expunge the event from my mind, as well as its loathsome consequences.

That smile. That grin. I was going to bring up my luncheon, then and there. I did. I do not know how I managed to walk home. The young girl helped me. I remember that when we arrived, I went directly up to our room and I spent the rest of the day in bed, with the curtains drawn.

For a very long span of time I felt trapped in a cell with no windows and no door. I could not find my way out. The place was dark and oppressive. For hours I tried to find the door, I was convinced it was hidden somewhere in the wallpaper's design, and I slid my palms and fingers along the walls, trying to find the crack of the door, desperate. This was not a dream. It rolled on in my mind, it endured as I went about my daily chores, looked after my children, my house, looked after you. Again and again the cell without any openings stifled me mentally. Sometimes I had to hide in the little cabinet behind our bedroom in order to breathe normally.

I never put my foot on the exact place where the deed had taken place, not far from where Madame Odette drew her last breath. Little by little I was able to obliterate the memory of what had happened in that room. It took months, it took years. My shining love for my son, my deep love for you, triumphed over the stark monstrosity of the truth. I never told you. I never could. As I stepped over the spot on the carpet day after day, I stepped over the memory. I blanked it out. I wiped it away, like one would a stain. How did I manage? How could I have endured it? I simply did. I squared my shoulders, like a soldier facing battle. The years rolled by. The horror faded. The carpet where it had happened also faded, until one day it was finally replaced.

Even today, my love, I cannot write the words, I cannot form the sentences that spell out the truth. I cannot. But the guilt has never stopped bearing down on me. And when Baptiste died, can you see now that I was convinced the Lord was punishing me for my sins?

When our son died, I tried to turn to Violette. She was my only child, now. But she never let me love her. She remained aloof, distant, slightly supercilious, as if she considered me less of a fine person than you. Now, with the distance that old age gives one, I see that she may have suffered from my preferring her brother. I see now that this was my greatest fault as a mother, loving Baptiste more than Violette, and showing it. How unfair this must have seemed to her. I always gave him the shiniest apple, the sweetest pear. He must have the seat in the shade, the softest bed, the best view at the theater, the umbrella if it was raining. Did he ever make the most of these advantages? Did he taunt his sister? Perhaps he did, unbeknownst. Perhaps he made her feel even more unloved.

I am trying to reflect upon all this calmly. My love for Baptiste was the most powerful force in my life. Were you convinced I could love only him? Did you also feel left out? I remember that once you did say something about my being besotted with the boy. I was. Oh, my love, I was. And when the hideous reality became evident, I loved him all the more. I could have loathed him, I could have rejected him, but no, my love surged even stronger, as if I had to desperately protect him from his frightful origins.

Remember how, after he died, I could not discard any of his belongings. For many years his room became a sort of shrine, a love temple to my adored boy. I would sit there in a kind of daze, and cry. You were gentle and kind, but you did not understand. How could you? Violette, growing into a young girl, despised my grief. Yes, I felt I was being punished. My golden prince had been taken away from me, because I had sinned, because I had not been able to prevent that assault. Because it had been my fault.

It is only now, Armand, as I hear the demolition team coming up the street, their loud voices, their crude laughter, their belligerence kindled by their horrific mission, that it seems the assault on me will take place again. This time, you see, it is not Monsieur Vincent who will bend me to his will, using his manhood as a weapon, no, it is a colossal snake of stone and cement that will crush the house to nothingness, that will propel me into oblivion. And behind that hideous snake of stone there is the one man in control. My enemy. That bearded man, that House Man. Him.

This house is like my body, it is like my own skin, my blood, my bones. It carries me like I have carried our children. It has been damaged, it has suffered, it has been violated, it has survived, but today, it will collapse. Today, nothing can save the house, nothing can save me. There is nothing out there, Armand, nothing or nobody that I wish to hold on to. I am an old lady now, it is time for me to take my leave.

After you died, a gentleman pursued me for a while. A respectable widower, Monsieur Gontrand, a jovial fellow with a paunch and long sideburns. He had taken quite a fancy to me. Once a week he paid his respects, with a small box of chocolates or a bunch of violets. I believe he also took a fancy to the house and to the income of the two shops. Ah, yes, your Rose is shrewd. His was a pleasurable company, I will concede. We played dominoes and cards, and I would offer him a glass of Madeira. He always left just before supper. After a while he became slightly more audacious. But he finally understood that I was not interested in becoming his wife. However, we remained friends over the years. I did not wish to remarry, like my mother did. Now that you are no longer here, I prefer being alone. I suppose only Alexandrine understands that. I must admit something more to you. She is the only person I will miss. I miss her now. I realize now that for all those years, after you left me, she gave me her friendship, and it was a priceless gift.

Oddly enough, in these final, awful moments, I find myself thinking about the Baronne de Vresse. Despite the age difference, the social one, I did feel we could have become friends. And I will readily confess that at one point I did ponder about using her connection with the Prefect to attract his attention, to save our house. Did she not attend his parties? Had he not once but twice come to the rue Taranne? But you see, I never did. I never dared. I respected her too much.

I think of her as I huddle down here, shivering, and I wonder if she has any inkling of what I am going through. I think of her in that beautiful, noble house, with her family, and her books and flowers and parties. Her porcelain tea set, her purple crinolines and her loveliness. The large, bright room where she would receive her guests. The sun dappling the glistening ancient floorboards. The rue Taranne is dangerously close to the new boulevard Saint-Germain. Will those sweet little girls grow up in another place? Would Louise Eglantine de Vresse bear to lose her family home standing proudly on the corner of the rue du Dragon? I will never know.

I think of my daughter waiting for me at Tours, wondering where I am. I think of Germaine, my loyal and trustworthy Germaine, who is undoubtedly worried at my absence. Has she guessed? Does she know I am hiding here? Every day they must wait for a letter, a sign, they must look up when they hear the stamp of hooves at the gate. In vain.

The last dream I had down here was a foreboding one. I do not quite know how to describe it to you. I was up in the sky, like a bird, looking down at our city. And it was only ruins that I saw. Charred ruins, glowing red, of a ravaged city, consumed by a vast fire. The Hôtel de Ville was burning like a torch, a huge, ghostlike carcass about to collapse. All the Prefect's work, all the Emperor's plans, all the symbols of their perfect, modern city had been annihilated. There was nothing left, only the desolation of the boulevards and their straight lines, cutting through embers like bleeding scars. Instead of sadness, a strange relief surged through me as the wind swept a black swarm of ashes my way. As I winged away, my nose and mouth full of cinders, I felt an unexpected elation take over. This was the end of the Prefect, the end of the Emperor. Even if it was only a dream, I had witnessed their downfall. And I savored it with relish.

They are now rattling about at the entrance. Crashes, bangs. My heart leaps. They are in the house, beloved. I hear them lumbering up and down the stairs, I hear their harsh voices ringing out into the empty rooms. I presume they want to make sure no one is here. I have closed the trapdoor to the cellar. I do not think they will find me because they will not care to look. They have received confirmation that the owners have vacated the premises. They are firmly convinced that Madame Veuve Armand Bazelet moved out a fortnight ago. The entire street is deserted. No one is living in the ghostlike row of houses, the last ones to be valiantly standing on the rue Childebert.

So they think. How many, like me? How many Parisians who will not surrender to the Prefect, to the Emperor? To so-called progress? How many Parisians hiding in their cellars because they will not give up their houses? I will never know.

They are coming down here. Footsteps thundering right over my head. I am writing this as fast as I can. Very scribbled handwriting. Perhaps I should blow the candle out! Can they see the flicker of the flame through the cracks in the wood? Oh, wait . . . They are already gone.

For a long while there is silence. Only the pounding of my heart and the scratch of quill on paper. It is a lugubrious wait. I am trembling from head to toe. I wonder what is going on. I dare not move from the cellar. From time to time, because otherwise I feel I shall go mad, I pick up a short novel called *Thérèse Raquin.* This was one of the last books Monsieur Zamaretti suggested before he left his shop. It is the lurid and fascinating tale of an adulterous, scheming couple. It is impossible to put it down. The writing is remarkably vivid, even more daring, I find, than Monsieur Flaubert's or Monsieur Poe's. Perhaps because it is so very modern? The author is a young man named Émile Zola. I believe he is not even thirty. The reaction to this book has been impressive. One journalist defined the novel as "putrid literature." Another claimed it was pornography. Few approved of it. Whatever one may think, this is a young author who will assuredly make his mark, one way or another.

How you must be surprised at me reading this. But you see, Armand, it is true to say that when one reads Monsieur Zola, one is brutally confronted with the worst aspects of human nature. There is nothing romantic about Monsieur Zola's writing. There is nothing noble about it either. For instance, the infamous scene at the town morgue (the establishment down by the river, where you and I had never gone to despite its growing popularity for visits by the public) is no doubt the most powerful piece of writing I have ever read in my entire life. It is even more macabre than what Monsieur Poe achieved. So how, you are surely wondering, can your meek, bland Rose approve of such literature? You may well ask. There is a dark side to your Rose. Your Rose has thorns.

Oh, suddenly I hear them perfectly, even from down here. I hear them clustering all over the house, a swarm of foul insects armed with pickaxes, and I make out the first blows, dreadfully sharp, up there on the roof. They attack the roof first, as you recall, then they work their way down. It will be a little while yet before they make their way down to me. But they will, eventually.

There is still time for me to flee. There is still time for me to rush up the stairs, unlock the trapdoor, the front door, and run out into the cold air. What a sight, an old woman in a dirty fur coat, her cheeks caked with grime. Another ragpicker, they will think. I am certain Gilbert is still out there, I am sure he is waiting for me, hoping against all hope that I will walk out that door.

I can still do it. I can still choose safety. I can let the house crumble down without me. I still have that choice. Listen, I am not a victim, Armand. This is what I want to do. Go down with the house. To be buried under it. Do you understand?

The noise is horrendous now. Each blow digging into slate, into stone, is like a blow delving into my bones, into my skin. I think of the church, placidly watching all this. The church will always be safe. It has witnessed bloodshed for centuries. Today will not make a difference. Who will know? Who will find me under the debris? At first I feared not being laid to rest by your side at the cemetery. Now I am convinced that it does not matter in the least if my remains are not next to yours. Our souls are already reunited.

I made you a promise and I will keep it. I

will not let that man have our empty house.

It is becoming very hard to write to you, my love. The dust is snaking its path down here. It is making me cough and wheeze. How long will this take? I wonder. Horrible creaks and groans now. The house shudders, like an animal in pain; like a ship caught on the crest of a frenzied storm.

It is unspeakable. I want to close my eyes. I want to think of the house as it used to be when you were still here, in all its glory, when Baptiste was alive, when we had guests coming in every week, when food was laid on the table, and the wine flowed, and laughter filled the room.

I think of our happiness, I think of the happy, simple life that is woven through these walls, the fragile tapestry of our existences. I think of the long, tall windows glowing out to me into the night when I used to make my way home from the rue des Ciseaux, a warm, beckoning light. And there you used to stand, waiting for me. I think of our doomed neighborhood, the simple beauty of the little streets stemming from the church that no one will remember.

Oh, there is someone fiddling with the trapdoor, my heart leaps as I scribble this to you in haste and panic. I refuse to leave, I will not leave. How can they have found me here? Who told them I was hiding? Shrieks, shouts, a high-pitched voice, screaming my name, over and over again. I dare not move. There is so much noise, I cannot make out who is calling . . . Is it? — the candle is flickering in the thick dust, I have nowhere to hide. Lord help me . . . I cannot breathe. Thunder overhead. There, the flame is out now, this is written in black-ness, in haste, in fear, someone is coming down . . .

Le Petit Journal, January 28th, 1869

A macabre discovery was made on the old rue Childebert, torn down for the creation of the new boulevard Saint-Germain. As workers shoveled through the rubble, they came upon the bodies of two women hidden in the cellar of one of the demolished houses . . . The women have been identified as Rose Cadoux, 59, widow of Armand Bazelet, and Alexandrine Walcker, 29, unmarried, who worked in a flower shop on the rue de Rivoli. It appears they were killed by the destruction of the house. The reason for these women's presence in an area that had been evacuated for the embellishments led by the Prefect's team has not yet been made clear. However, Madame Bazelet was granted an interview last summer by the Hôtel de Ville where it was noted that she had not agreed to move out of her property. Madame Bazelet's daughter, Madame Laurent Pesquet, from Tours, claimed she had been expecting her mother for the past three weeks. When reached by our journalist, the Préfecture's legal counsel replied that the Prefect had no comment whatsoever to make concerning the matter.

ABOUT THE AUTHOR

Tatiana de Rosnay is the author of ten novels, including the *New York Times* best-selling novel *Sarah's Key,* an international sensation with over 5 million copies sold in 38 countries worldwide that has now been made into a major film. Together with Dan Brown and Stieg Larsson, she was named one of the top three fiction writers in Europe in 2010. Tatiana lives with her husband and two children in Paris.

The employees of Thorndike Press hope you have enjoyed this Large Print book. All our Thorndike, Wheeler, and Kennebec Large Print titles are designed for easy reading, and all our books are made to last. Other Thorndike Press Large Print books are available at your library, through selected bookstores, or directly from us.

For information about titles, please call:
  (800) 223-1244

or visit our Web site at:
  http://gale.cengage.com/thorndike

To share your comments, please write:
  Publisher
  Thorndike Press
  10 Water St., Suite 310
  Waterville, ME 04901